SEXY BEAST

PIPER RAYNE

Cover design: MadHat Covers

Model: Jacob Rodney

Photographer: Wander Aguilar

Line Editor: Love N Books

Proof Reader: Shawna Gavas, Behind The Writer

About Sexy Beast

It's time.

Time to get a life.
Time to start over.
Time to move beyond the past.

The guys in the Single Dads Club would tell you it was time years ago, but until recently, the risk of hurting my little girl outweighed the benefit of getting a piece of ass.

Now that I have a tween daughter on my hands? It's becoming more apparent with every poster hung on the wall, every fight over make-up and every uncomfortable conversation about puberty, that at least one of us needs a female touch in our lives.

Jesus. I can't even think the words 'female touch' without thinking of *her*.

Charlotte Rose. Charlie.

She's everything I shouldn't want, but someone needs to tell that to my damn libido because every time she's around I have a constant case of blue balls.

There's a list of reasons why I shouldn't give into what I feel—she's my best friend's little sister, she's seen me at my most vulnerable, and the biggest one—she's the first person in eleven years who has the potential to break me.

Sexy BEAST

DEDICATION

To all the women who love the strong silent type with a
heart of gold.

1

GARRETT

Another damn fundraiser.

I sit, taking it all in with my ass in a chair, drinking some new IPA my buddy, Dane, just put on the menu at Happy Daze Tavern. Every time I come to one of these, I'm transported back to when I was the guest of honor all those years ago, front and center with a new baby in my arms. They propped me up there like show and tell with Sydney, only two months old, cradled in my arms. We hadn't even bonded at that point—I was too busy grieving. Too busy drowning in despair for the both of us.

I tip my beer as a hello to Hank from Nail Me Hardware then go back to staring down my now twelve-year-old daughter, watching as she twirls her hair while talking with a boy. Is that maneuver bred into girls or is it ingrained in their DNA? I remember Melissa doing it the first time I met her.

The boy needs to learn what a pair of jeans *should* look like. They damn well shouldn't be tight around the ankles and his shirt...whatever happened to T-shirts with sports teams or sportswear logos? They've been replaced with plain V-neck T-shirts that fit like a second skin. No twelve-year-old boy has the muscles to fill out a shirt like that, let alone Xander, the kid flirting with my daughter.

"Why so glum?" Charlie, the bartender and MC of tonight's fundraiser plops down in the chair next to me.

I down a swig of my beer, eyeing her over the rim of the bottle.

"Ah...the boy." She follows my line of sight to the table my daughter is now leaning over. If that little shit so much as tries to look down her shirt, he's toast. "You going to knock him out?" she asks.

I shift my gaze away from my daughter, back to Charlie Rose. Charlotte is her real name, but as long as I've known her, which is close to birth, she's been Charlie. She grew up in this town with her three older brothers, one being my best friend. Well, my best friend until he moved to Los Angeles to live the bachelor life while I continued to raise my daughter solo. All in all, he's a good guy. The entire Rose family was my second family growing up.

"You're unusually chipper tonight," I comment and take another swig of my beer.

"Well, I'm happy that Ava will be able to re-open the bakery." She crosses her legs and the small table for two leaves me plenty of room to notice how slender they are.

Charlie grew up years ago. Her breasts developed, her hips expanded, and that tomboy I knew growing up who followed me and her brother Vance around transformed into a beautiful woman.

"I saw your donation. Very nice," she says.

I nod again and study the label of my beer bottle to stop myself from checking out her legs again.

A long, drawn out sigh leaves her lips. "If you're that bothered by it, go over there and ask her to stop."

Did I mention, Charlie expresses her opinions?

Openly?

All the time?

The only time I enjoy it is when she's giving Dane shit for something.

"So she can hate me?"

"She'll never hate you. You're her dad," she says.

I blow out a long breath and roll my eyes just like Sydney does to me constantly these days.

"You don't get it." I down the rest of my beer, raising my hand for the waitress.

"No waitresses, remember? Fundraiser." She stands, grabs my bottle and disappears.

Now that I'm alone with my thoughts again, I appraise my daughter who is now sitting back down in her chair, fiddling with her phone, while jackass Xander is doing the same. The difference is, I can't see Sydney's face and Xander has a teasing smile on his. It reminds me of some douche in a locker room bragging about his latest conquest.

I rub my eyes. I have to calm down. She's twelve, not sixteen.

A cold beer is placed in front of me. A Budweiser, my beer of choice.

Charlie plops herself back down at my table.

"Thanks."

"No problem." She shrugs.

Cat bounces over to the table with six-year-old Lily right next to her. "So, you ready to start?" she asks Charlie, then gives me a sweet half-smile.

Cat is my buddy, Marcus', girlfriend, Lily his daughter from another woman. They fell in love this past summer and I can't deny that I'm a little envious of him. Not that I'd want to put an 'available now' sign on my heart after my wife Melissa's passing, but it's the moments I see them share sometimes when I miss her the most.

The soft kisses they think they're sneaking, or the hand holding on the way out to the car. Hell, even when he opens the door and pulls out the chair for her. I'm not one hundred percent sure it's the act itself or her soft smile and loving eyes I'd receive in return I miss the most.

Charlie hops to her feet. Always ready to pounce on whatever needs to be done.

"I'll be back."

I tip my beer in her direction, my gaze shifting back to Syd, finding her by herself, her thumbs flying across the screen of her phone.

It isn't until Charlie's up on stage, under the lights, announcing the first donation to be auctioned off, that I realize the curves of her body have transformed her into a full woman now, which means that honoring her brother's wishes of making sure she ends up with a good guy is going to be even harder for me now.

I shift in my seat trying to get comfortable refusing to believe that my dick is in full chub mode right now because of the girl whose pigtails I used to pull to try to drive her crazy when she was younger.

I SIT FOR ANOTHER HALF HOUR, SIPPING A BEER AND MAKING small talk when I'm forced to. My sour mood has lifted slightly since Xander is now in the arcade with his friends and Syd is surrounded by her friends.

Charlie and Cat are both up on stage trying to get everything organized before the guest of honor arrives.

Charlie approaches the microphone, her eyes wide and matching her smile.

Jumping off the stage, she rushes past me and the crowd follows her back to find Dane and the guest of honor, Ava Pearson. The two look cozy so they must've made up. Dane's son, eight-year-old Toby, is asleep in his arms.

After everyone has said their hellos and Ava doesn't appear as stunned as she did when she first arrived, Cat's voice sounds out through the microphone.

"Should we get started?" Everyone's attention is drawn off the couple and up to her on the stage. "The first auction item up for grabs is a two night stay in a real log cabin, generously donated by our very own Garrett Shaw."

Her hand extends my way, and I reluctantly fold myself out of the chair and walk up to the makeshift stage. A tight smile and my hand smoothing down my beard is about all the audience is going to get from me.

"Let's start the bidding at one hundred dollars." The words are barely out of Cat's mouth when Charlie's hand flies up.

"One thousand!" Charlie shouts out. The smile on her face would make you think she just won a grand, not spent it. Something I know she can't afford.

"Sold!" Cat hits the gavel on the lecture pedestal in front of her denying anyone else a chance to bid.

My head turns in Charlie's direction. She's smiling ear to ear, almost bouncing on the balls of her feet.

What the hell is she thinking?

Cat looks over her shoulder at me, her smile matching Charlie's. What the hell is going on?

I leave the stage and push through the crowd, my determined footsteps echoing out as I make my way to the back of the room and the curly haired girl I'm not going to let waste her money.

"Take it easy on her," Dane says under his breath as I bypass him, dragging Charlie by the arm toward the bathrooms.

"Stop it," Charlie demands, and twists her elbow out of my hold.

"What are you doing?"

"Supporting my best friend." She presses her back up against the wall. I don't miss the way her generously proportioned tits strain against her Happy Daze T-shirt. Dane probably tells her to wear it tight with the hopes that his male customers will buy more drinks. Then again, no one really tells Charlie to do anything.

"There's no way you can afford it." I lean in closer, lowering my voice. "If you wanted to stay in one of my cabins I would have let you. You just had to ask."

"That's not the point." She crosses her arms over her chest, effectively making them that much more enticing to any man in a five-mile radius. "And for your information, I have the money. Not that it's any of your business."

She pushes off the wall, her eyes narrowed slits as she stares me down before she takes a step away.

"I'll pay the thousand dollars for you and you can stay at the cabin."

Her head slowly twists in my direction and for a second it's almost eerie—the way she looks like a robot with how calculated her moves are. "You certainly will not. I'm not some little girl you know. I'm not the baby sister of your best friend who's too immature to make a rational decision for herself."

Words of agreement almost leave my mouth. Especially

after she turns on her heels and walks away. No guy could argue that her ass is definitely that of a grown woman.

The self-loathing I'm all too familiar with when it comes to Charlie Rose bears down on me and I remind myself...

She's your best friend's little sister.

You promised to watch out for her.

She's young and free, what the fuck would she want with you?

Most of all, I'm damaged. Damaged goods. And she is the perfect package and should stay that way.

I PULL UP TO MY LATEST CABIN ON FOXFIELD TRAIL, MY biggest project yet. Eight bedrooms, seven bathrooms, a pool, a weight room, wrap around deck. It's for multi-families, blended families or just one big ass family. When I had the plans drawn up for it, I thought it was going to be spectacular—instead it's been a pain in my ass.

The permits, the inspections, the investment. Nothing has gone according to plan and when you add on the fact that one of my best subcontractors just ran away with his girlfriend to start a new life elsewhere, you guessed it, I'm about a month behind schedule.

A month behind for Jasper Banks, a client who refers me out like a coke dealer. He and his wife, Lennon, wanted to be the first to occupy the cabin. They're hosting a family reunion for his wife's side of the family. I've got until two days before Christmas to get the cabin habitable, otherwise, I'm screwed since all my other cabins are already booked.

"George," I approach the man who took over my last sub's job.

He wipes his greasy hands on his worn T-shirt that says, Muscles Under Construction.

"Garrett," he nods and smiles at me, but his voice is on alert.

George is about twenty years my senior. He's from the neighboring town of Wet Rock and started his own company only six months ago after his boss, my ex-subcontractor ran off.

"Where is everyone?" I ask, looking around at an empty cabin that is far from finished.

"We have a few issues." He wipes his hands on his T-shirt again.

Of course we do. Never once have I walked into this house and not heard that phrase.

"What?" I run my hand down my beard. Most men lose hair on their head, I lose hair on my beard. Especially since starting this cabin.

"Nothing too major," he stalls.

"Tell me."

George drops the pen he's trying to slip back into his pocket. He's flustered and my stomach clenches waiting for his response.

"The hot tub is on backorder."

"Until?" If George wasn't already so flustered I might grab him by that T-shirt and tug him toward me, but I already scare the crap out of him and the last thing I need is for him to leave me stranded at this point. So, I handle him like I do Syd—with gentle hands.

"Three months." His gaze shoots to the side.

My head falls back and I tuck my hands in my pockets. "Options?"

"You head into Portland or San Francisco, pick another one out, but..."

"But what, George?"

He drops his pen again. "It's also all the tubs and sinks in the house, too."

I rub my hand down my beard. "How exactly is that possible?"

"The ones you picked are all made by the same company and all the employees went on strike."

I shake my head, thinking of what to do. Everything was special ordered. "Okay, how far does that push us back?"

"I need measurements of the new stuff before my guys can install the floor and tile." His gaze continues to play hide and seek with me, never truly meeting mine.

"Fine. I'll figure it out today."

My phone rings in my pocket.

"Syd," I mumble, holding it out in my hand. I raise my finger to stop George's rambling before I accept the call. "What's up, Syd?"

"Dad," she doesn't say anything else, but the soft tremble in her voice starts my heart racing.

"What is it?"

"Um..."

"Syd!" my voice goes up another octave.

"I, um..."

My hand runs down my beard and I'm sure another bunch of hair must sprinkle to the floor.

"Are you okay?" I ask, desperate to know what's going on.

"Yeah. I um, I..."

"Do you need me?"

"I got my period," she blurts out.

I'm momentarily stunned but my heart apparently got the message because my heart rate skyrockets like I was just shot out of a cannon.

I angle my body away from George. "Period?" I whisper into the phone.

"Yeah, and I need some things."

Fuck. I can't deny I've thought about this moment before, known it had to be coming at some point soon, but for whatever reason, I never pictured myself at the store buying them for her.

"Okay, okay, I can do that." I may be trying to convince myself that I can handle this more than her.

"The nurse is out...please Dad." My baby girl's voice is really trembling now. This is the first time in forever that I've felt like she truly needed me. I can't screw this up.

Long gone are the days of rescuing her from the monkey bars when she was scared to jump, or holding her bike as she learned to ride on two wheels. Lately, my only use to her has been to pay for her cell phone and feed her stomach.

"I'll be right there," I say.

"Okay."

We hang up and I don't bother explaining to George where I'm headed as I walk toward the door of the cabin.

"So, you'll let me—"

I put my hand in the air. "I've got it handled, George."

I walk out the front door of the cabin with one mission, to save my baby girl, but that was before I knew there were so many choices in the feminine product aisle.

2

CHARLIE

I tap my shoes along the linoleum floor to the beat of the song that was on the radio when I drove into work. All's quiet in Climax Cove Middle School at the moment since class is in session. I don't know why the former counselor, Mrs. Quentin decided to leave her husband and run off with Mr. Ashland, the town fix-it man, and although I feel horrible for Mr. Quentin, having a permanent counseling job after floating between schools on a part-time basis is awesome.

The problem is, Mrs. Quentin must have been too busy tending to her affair because she's kept no records of the kids she's talked to. There are no notes anywhere regarding the students who need special assistance. For the last two days, I've sat at my desk, scouring every inch of her office and come up empty.

My phone rings, saving me from finalizing my fifth paperclip chain.

"Hey Lori," I answer, seeing on the screen that it's the secretary from the front office calling.

"Miss Rose, there's a father up here."

I sit up straighter in my chair like I'm a puppy and Lori's holding my leash. Practically salivating for something to do.

"I'll be right there." I hang up but hear her saying something else.

She can tell me in two minutes when I reach her.

The main office is like a fishbowl-windows on three of the four walls, which makes it easy to see the big strapping, Garrett Shaw talking with Lori and holding a bag at his side. The mere sight of him sets my entire body on fire.

Garrett Shaw has been my brother's best friend since, I don't know, maybe birth. I think I've loved him since I was old enough to crush on a boy, but to him, I'm like a little sister. Not that it matters—after Garrett lost his high school sweetheart wife, he's never been the same. Not at all like the boy I fell in love with. When she died, that wild and funny piece of him was buried, too.

I open the door to the office.

"Here she is, Mr. Shaw," Lori holds out her hand in my direction. "I think you remember Charlotte Rose, right?"

Garrett slowly turns round, the plastic bag in his hand crinkling as he squeezes it tighter.

"Charlie," he says my name like I'm still twelve.

"Hey, Garrett." My eyes shoot to the bag, assuming it must be something for his daughter.

"Garrett needs to deliver something to Sydney," Lori says when Garrett stands there unspeaking.

I got called away from my world record paperclip chain to be a messenger. Great way to put my Master's degree to work.

I hold my hand out for the bag. "Sure. I think Sydney is in Science right now. I can bring it to her."

Garrett doesn't so much as move a muscle in an effort to pass me the bag.

"I'd like to give it to her myself."

My hand falls back down to my side. "Lori, can you page Mr. Trickle and tell him to send Sydney down?"

Lori nods and picks up the phone.

Garrett stands there in his jeans and flannel shirt, looking like the lumberman he is. The man has earned the respect he gets in this town after starting and managing a log cabin building business that's kept many men and women in this town working. Sometimes he sells them to rich folk and others he keeps and rents out.

Lori hangs up the phone and then scratches her head with a pen. "So, Garrett, all the cabins booked for Christmas?"

Garrett smiles but it doesn't quite reach his eyes. He's stressed about something and I hope it isn't about the cabins. Shaw's Cabins are one of the businesses that keep the town afloat during the after-summer slump. People travel down from Portland and up from San Francisco to rent his cabins throughout the winter. Rumor is that the owner of Hart's Desire Products and her husband are one of Garrett's biggest clients, but since it's Garrett, his lips always remain sealed.

"We are."

Silence commences and I rock back on my heels, my hands shoved into the pockets of my slacks.

I spot Sydney walking down the hall a few minutes later, doing some sort of strange waddle to the office with her legs locked together from the knees up.

I'm not bragging but my counselor skills assess the situation quickly, figuring out exactly what Garrett is bringing her.

A laugh slips out of me, but my hand flies up to my mouth. No chance.

The rough and gruff Garrett Shaw is bringing his daughter maxi pads.

When the door opens and Sydney walks in about to burst into tears, my laughter subsides. As funny as it is that Garrett has to deal with this situation, I'm sure Sydney is terrified.

"Dad," Sydney says with relief.

"Hey, Syd." He wraps his arm around her and she seems to find refuge in his embrace.

"Would the two of you like to come to my office?" I suggest to get them away from Lori and the other office ladies and so I can see if Sydney has any questions she needs answered.

"No, I'll be fine." Sydney pulls away, grabbing the bag from his hands.

I glimpse into the bag as it passes in front of me and what I find leaves me wide-eyed and wanting to laugh again.

Garrett, Garrett, Garrett.

"No, I really think you should both come with me." I walk to the door, not willing to take no for an answer, holding it open for both of them.

Surprisingly, they follow without further argument. What little I know of Sydney is that she's very much like her father—no one tells her what to do. Just two weeks ago, she kneed a kid in the nuts for some reason she refused to divulge to the principal.

We reach my office a couple of minutes later. "Please take a seat. I'll be right back."

I head to the nurse's office a few doors down. Nurse Wendy called in sick today and since this is a small school district, I'm responsible for filling in for her where I can. Rifling through her cabinets, I pull out a few maxi pads and head back into my office.

The two are sitting there in silence.

I take the bag from Sydney's hands and pass the maxi pads to her. She rewards me with a small smile.

"Charlie, I already got her what she needs," Garrett says, sounding a little annoyed.

I pull the package he brought out of the plastic bag. "Garrett, adult diapers are not what women use for their period."

"Ew," Sydney cries out, her head twisting in her dad's direction with a horrified look on her face. "Seriously, Dad?"

Garrett's cheeks redden along the line of his beard. He shrugs. "I thought that was the right thing to get."

Sydney stands and tucks the pads into her pocket. "I have to get to Science."

"I can take you home," Garrett offers. "Shouldn't you be resting?"

I bite my lip.

Professional counselor, not barmaid. Don't mix my daytime and night time job up.

By some miracle, I manage to hold in my sarcastic comment.

"I'm fine," Sydney bites out.

Garrett stands, towering over his daughter. "I don't know Syd, maybe you should just come home so you can lay on the couch the rest of the day."

Sydney completely disregards his comment and focuses on me. "Thank you, Miss Rose. I'll see you at home, Dad."

Then she leaves.

She leaves me alone with Garrett.

I'm not sure when the last time I was alone in a room with him was...that fateful night when he came home with my brother? When I thought for sure he saw me as more than just a baby sister?

He turns his attention to me and all the air rushes from my lungs. Many people are intimidated by Garrett Shaw—whether it's because of his gruff nature, his six-foot-six statue, or his muscles stacked upon muscles—I'm not sure. But for me, it's the opposite.

He doesn't intimidate me, he brings out my school girl crush, which is just as terrifying.

He runs his hands down his beard, a habit I've noticed he does when he's upset. "I can't do anything right."

"She's a preteen. Get used to it."

I round my desk and put the adult diapers back into the bag, handing it to him.

"It seemed to happen overnight. One day I was pushing her on the swings and the next she's slamming her door in my face."

He accepts the bag, although I doubt he's going to return them to the store.

"Well, be patient with her. Hormones make girls crazy." I giggle, remembering that night when he blamed my actions on hormones.

You don't really want me. It's just those girly hormones making you think you do," he'd said to me.

His gaze shoots to mine, a smile peeking through the beard surrounding his luscious lips.

"You're right. It's almost like you're not yourself?" He poses it as a question and I lean against my desk, quickly grabbing a pen to fiddle with.

Does he want me to say no? Hormones were part of me wanting him of course, but I decide the better thing is to ignore his question altogether.

"She'll grow up just fine. You've done great this far, keep it up, big guy."

He stares at me for an uncomfortable minute and then nods. "Thanks for your help, Charlie."

"What about that cabin?" I throw the question out there because I don't want him to leave. I like having him here.

Garrett shakes his head. "Let me know when you want it, but I paid the grand to Dane already."

Now him leaving doesn't upset me.

"You what?" I ask, my voice rising. "I told you I'd pay it."

He turns on his heels, his frame taking up the entire height and width of my door.

"I told you, I'd pay it. You don't need to spend your money on that. We're practically family."

"Just because you're best friends with Vance doesn't make us family. Here." I round the corner of my desk, pulling out my purse and my checkbook.

"I don't want the money, Charlie." He stays in the doorway with his hands above his head holding onto the door frame and jeez, the way it makes the muscles in his arms bunch and stretches the flannel shirt he's wearing is really distracting.

But no. I'm annoyed with him right now. He's acting like a stubborn mule.

I scribble out the check, tear it off and I'm on way toward him when he turns around and walks out of my office, down the hall.

"Garrett!" I chase after him.

He shakes his head, those long strides increasing the distance between us.

Principal Hayes picks that exact moment to exit the office. "Mr. Shaw, how nice to see you again," he says.

Principal Rich Hayes, Richy Rich as people refer to him because his family was the founders of this town. They live in the biggest house downtown and they're always on floats in every parade.

Garrett holds out his hand. "Hey, Rich, gotta run. Call me."

Rich glances over to me from the corner of his eye.

"Mr. Shaw please wait," I say, disregarding Principal Hayes.

Garrett goes through the doors and I follow, catching him outside.

"Seriously, Garrett, what are you eight?"

He stops and spins around.

"Charlie, I don't want your money. I made a promise to Vance years ago when he left that I'd take care of you. This is me sticking to my word."

My fucking brother, Vance and his notion that his baby sister can't take care of herself.

I fold the check up and stick it in his front pocket.

"I don't need you to take care of me. I'm a grown woman." I stick out my breasts for him to see how serious I am. "Or hadn't you noticed?"

His gaze dips down to my cleavage and his chest rises and falls with a deep breath. Then, a mask of indifference washes over his face. He nods and walks toward his truck, throwing the adult diapers in the bed of Principal Hayes' pickup truck before he gets into his vehicle and speeds away without a backward glance.

3

A few weeks later my keys are in my hands, and I'm searching for my phone when Sydney walks downstairs. I'm late to the Single Dads Club meeting and that's probably why she's ventured out of her cave. She thought I'd be gone by now.

"Syd, have you seen my phone?" I continue to search the couch cushions, although I haven't sat on it from the time I walked in the door until now.

"No." She opens the kitchen cabinet, rummaging through its contents.

"I can grab dinner on my way home."

"I'm not really hungry," she says, and then comes out of the kitchen with a bag of tortilla chips and a jar of salsa. "It was in the fridge." She throws me my phone with her other hand.

Good thing my rugby skills are still awesome.

I catch it and eye her chips. "Hungry for crap though?"

She shrugs, and heads to the couch, plopping down on our brown leather sofa and putting her feet up on the table.

"I'm still bringing home dinner. You can pretend you're hungry." I tuck my phone into my pocket.

"Have a good meeting complaining about me." She smiles over her full mouth of chips. How did I raise such a smart ass? You'd think she's related to my buddy Dane, not me.

"You know that's not the point of the meeting."

"Since I don't go on many play dates these days and I don't need a babysitter, so I have to wonder what you *do* talk about there." She flips the channel onto her Netflix account.

"Nothing inappropriate," I say, nodding toward the television.

"Okay," she pretends to sulk. "I see you're still employing the do as I say, not as I do parenting technique."

"Smart ass." I shake my head and she laughs.

My heart warms. Nothing better than hearing the sound of her amusement, it's so foreign these days.

"Case in point. Swear jar is on the table."

I miss our playful banter. It's nice to have her out of her room for once. Lately, I feel as alone as I did after Melissa died, what with Sydney spending so much time in her room.

"I might stop by the Mad Batter. Do you want me to bring you home a cupcake?"

"Unicorn one, please," she smiles over another mouthful of chips.

I nod and turn to walk to the front door. "Aren't I the parent of the month? Chips and cupcakes for dinner." My hand lands on the doorknob.

"Don't beat yourself up. I brushed my teeth and showered today."

My smile grows and a small part of me doesn't want to go to the Single Dads Club meeting because times like this are rare, but I'm not so naive to think she's going to cuddle into my side and watch a movie with me either.

"Good to know I did something right."

I open the door to our cabin, the sky already growing dark this early in the evening because of winters approach.

"Hey," she calls out after me and I turn around. "You did a great job."

Did I just enter an alternate universe? Maybe I'm dreaming.

"Thank you."

"Don't thank me, I'm just trying to butter you up so you don't complain about me at the meeting." She giggles and I shake my head, shutting the door.

It's small moments like this one that gives me hope that I'm not completely screwing up this single parenting thing.

***

THE SINGLE DADS CLUB MEETINGS ARE HELD AT MY BUDDY'S bar, Happy Daze Tavern which is located in small downtown Climax Cove. I park my truck along the sidewalk behind Charlie's lime green Jeep. I'm not sure why she'd pick such a horrible color, but Charlie has always marched to the beat of her own drum.

Other members are already milling about inside and most wave a hello to me as I make my way to the bar to grab a drink.

Charlie's dropping an orange slice into my other buddy, Marcus' beer. The man loves his Blue Moon. Yuppie drink if you ask me.

"Hey," I lean my arms on the bar.

"I heard a rumor about you," Marcus says, wearing a shit-eating smirk.

My gaze shoots over to Charlie who is waiting for me to give her my drink order.

She holds her hands up in the air. "Wasn't me."

Her hair is pulled back into a ponytail but a few stray hairs have escaped, their curls framing her face. Jesus, why do I notice shit like that about her?

Marcus glances between the two of us, some expression I can't name crossing his face.

"There's the old man." Dane enters from the back room, his girlfriend Ava following behind him. Straightening her blouse.

"Seriously? I challenge you guys to last one afternoon," Charlie hollers and Marcus laughs next to me.

"They couldn't last from breakfast to lunch," he challenges.

Dane waits for Ava and then pulls her into his arms. "Don't be jealous that I'm so irresistible she can't go more than a couple of hours without me."

Ava rolls her eyes. "Switch that around, babe. I'm the irresistible one."

Dane's head falls back in laughter. "That you are." He grabs her hand. "Let's go back to the office, one more time."

She smacks his stomach. "I have to get back to the bakery. Cat is probably wondering what took me so long."

Charlie takes a break from wiping down the counter. "She's not an idiot, she knows what took you so long."

"Nice that you use my girlfriend to cover work for you while you two get some play." Marcus shakes his head, although the smile on his face says he's not serious.

"Lily enjoys pushing those cupcakes," Dane replies with mock offense.

"And Cat offered," Ava adds. "If you don't like it maybe you shouldn't have worked so hard to get my bakery back up and running." Ava sticks her tongue out at Marcus like a three-year-old and he chuckles.

I remain quiet, not having a ton to add because I am now the only single one of this three-man crew. So, most nights where they'd come over to watch the latest boxing match or Monday Night football, they now spend with their girl-friends.

It's like high school all over again when pussy is more important than the boys. What the hell am I talking about? Pussy should still be more important than the boys. I just don't have any pussy to nail.

My gaze shoots to Charlie again, and then down in front of me, finding me a beer in a tall frosted glass.

"Try it. Something different." She nudges it my way.

"IPA?" I ask.

"No. I said something different."

Charlie ventures down the bar to another single dad waiting for a drink. I think his name is Eddie, he was new last month. He says something funny and she laughs while grabbing his drink.

He slides his credit card over the bar and she takes it to the register to ring him up. His eyes zoom in on her ass. The jeans she's wearing shows off how great of an ass she has and even though I can't really blame him, my hand tightens around the glass anyway.

"Are you going to try it?" Marcus elbows me.

I snap my attention away from her ass and bring the beer to my lips. It's got a nice flavor to it, so I sip more. "It's good," I remark.

Charlie peers over her shoulder at me, her hand resting on the credit card receipt holder. "Told you." She smiles proudly, one that says you should listen to me more often.

"So, what is this I hear about you buying adult diapers?

Having bladder control issues already, old man?" Dane's hand lands on my shoulder and he can barely get the question out without laughing.

I shake my head. "Fucking Frida at Munchies Corner Store."

"You know to head outside city limits for shit like that." Dane rounds the bar now, grabbing a beer himself.

"Don't forget to pay the till, boss." Charlie reminds him and he pulls a bill out of his pocket and hands it over to her.

"Cheeps. No tip." Charlie and Dane have an unusual relationship for employee and boss. The casual observer would guess that Charlie was his sister rather than his employee.

"You want a tip?" He wraps his arms around her and presses his lips to her cheek in an exaggerated way.

"Ew." She wipes her face with her hand and wipes the saliva on his face. "Keep your germs to yourself."

I watch the ease and playfulness of their relationship and I'm not going to lie, the green monster twitches inside me.

Charlie's gaze flicks to mine after their exchange and I don't turn away like I usually do. I can't. She was rocking a professional look earlier, but I prefer her the way she is right now—in jeans and T-shirt with her hair pulled away from her face. Natural Charlie is so much sexier.

"Okay, get going. We'll talk about your diapers later, big guy," Dane jokes as he finishes up with something behind the bar.

"In all seriousness, why were you buying them? For your parents?" Marcus asks as we make our way to the big table we gather around for our meetings.

Not likely. My parents are still off on their once-in-a-life-time trip around the world. Just wait until they return home in nine months and find out about all the changes their granddaughter has undergone.

"Sydney got her period," I say, knowing she'd secretly be cursing me if she knew I just announced it.

"Oh shit." Marcus takes his fist and bites down. His daughter, Lily, is years away from being a preteen but he's scared of it, I know.

"Yeah, and I had to bring her something to school."

"And you bought her adult diapers?" Marcus cocks his head to the side.

"Well, I figured—"

"Even I know the difference."

I let the comment go, but the last woman that used any products for their period died twelve years ago. Melissa was insistent on her privacy, shutting the door when she went to the bathroom and keeping her feminine products at the back of the cabinet. The only time I knew she had her period was when she'd tell me we *can't* have sex tonight.

Dane finally sits down and the meeting begins. The usual frustrations and stories are shared around the table for an hour and when it's all said and done I place an order for take-out. After the meeting, I remain at the table to chat with Marcus and Dane until the food is ready.

Ava comes in with a box, placing it on the table in front of me.

"These are for Sydney." She winks and then turns around, wiggling out of Dane's reach and heads over to Charlie.

"Thanks."

"It's a girl thing," she hollers over her shoulder and I look down at the box, finding a unicorn one, but the other three are all chocolate.

"Is that peanut butter and chocolate?" Dane leans over

to get a look inside the box. He's mildly obsessed with his girlfriend's cupcakes. "Babe!" he yells after her.

"I have your box at the shop." She never looks his way.

"You know how to take care of your man," he says back.

"What girl thing is she talking about?" He turns his attention back to the box.

"Syd got her period." Marcus fills him in since I didn't mention it at the meeting because I'm not someone to share that kinda shit. Her attitude and flirting with boys sure, but the fact she's changing into a woman, hell to the no. I don't even want to acknowledge it myself.

"Oh fuck." Dane cringes.

"That's why the adult diapers fiasco," Marcus informs him again.

Charlie comes over and drops off another round of beers.

"Come on man, you didn't." Dane's bellow of laughter rings out through the entire bar.

"He did."

Fuck these two. Wait until they have to deal with this shit.

"I'm out," I say, irritation lacing my words.

"Wait, wait, wait," Dane calms down from his hysterical laughing. "We need to do something for her. This is like a monumental moment in her life."

Huh, I hadn't thought about it that way so much as I've been thinking how much this changes my life. Period means womanhood. Womanhood means growing up. Growing up means sex.

Nope.

Not going there.

"Like what? A party?" Marcus asks and Dane slaps the table.

"Exactly. Like an 'I am woman hear me roar' party."

"A period party?" I ask. "I'm not sure, she doesn't like a lot of attention."

"Yes, a period party! Ava can make some sort of cake in celebration. I'm sure Cat can decorate and we'll invite her friends. It's like a coming out except it will be like I am woman hear me roar type of theme." Dane's gaze focuses far away and I know his mind is going crazy with ideas.

Is this what I should be doing for my little girl? I guess it would show her that I support her as she heads into this next phase of her life.

"I *could* invite her close friends," I muse.

"You should invite boys, too." Dane glances behind him and I follow his line of sight to see Ava and Charlie standing by the bar with their mouths dropped open.

"You think?" I ask.

"I'm with Garrett, I'm not sure you want the boys there. Do you really want to be advertising to all the horny preteens that your daughter is a woman now?" Marcus cringes.

"It's like a bat mitzvah." Dane stands and approaches his girlfriend, the town's Mad Batter. "What do you think you could do for a design? A vulva? Maybe a red velvet cake?" At least he laughs at that.

"I am *not* making a cake," she says.

"You guys are being ridiculous," Charlie calls out from the bar, her back facing me. "No girl would ever want a period party."

"I think you're wrong," Dane argues. "Who doesn't love having a party thrown for them?"

"An adolescent girl who just got her period," Ava chimes in.

Charlie turns around and stares me directly in the eye.

"You throw her this party and I'd sleep with one eye open." Her lack of smile or joking demeanor voice tells me she's dead serious.

"I'm not exactly on the list of Sydney's favorite people these days, so I think I'll listen to Charlie."

Charlie smiles sweetly over at me and my stomach stirs.

"She has no idea what she's talking about." Dane waves her off.

"Yeah, babe, she's only a counselor and a woman." Ava rolls her eyes. "You're a bar owner and a reformed man whore so you must be right."

Dane picks her up, swinging her over his shoulder. "Woman, you argue with me and you get punished." He carries her down the hall as she hits him in the back while laughing like she's having the time of her life.

"I gotta get home to Cat and Lily. Sorry about the news, man. Though I know I'll be there soon enough." Marcus clasps my shoulder. "See ya, Charlie."

He leaves and then the bar is quiet and I'm left with Charlie.

"I better get going, I'm picking up food for Sydney."

Charlie nods. "Night, Garrett." She smiles and turns her attention back to the cash register.

I take one step toward the door but hesitate for a second.

"Thank you for today, Charlie. I'm in foreign territory with Sydney. I appreciate you rescuing me."

She grants me her attention, that sweet smile still on her lips, but this time it reaches her eyes. "If you need anything else, I suggest you come to me instead of Dane."

I nod. "I'll do that. Have a good night."

"You too," she says and turns around again.

As I walk out the door of the bar, something feels amiss but I can't put my finger on it.

4

———

CHARLIE

I sit at my desk at school, tapping my pen, waiting for a copy of the yearbook from two thousand and one to appear on my computer screen.

Why do I care?

Why am I torturing myself?

Maybe it was the way he smiled at me last night. Or how he really seemed to appreciate my help with Sydney. Did that spur the small hope that maybe he's ready to move on from her?

The yearbook comes up and there's his class on the cover. Climax Cove isn't a huge town so you can imagine how small our graduating class is.

His arm is slung over Melissa's shoulders, his clean-shaven face showcasing his wide smile confirming how happy he was with her. My finger clicks the mouse and scrolls through the digital copy of the yearbook and page after page—Garrett or Melissa are plastered all over this thing. It might as well be called 'Class of Two Thousand and One: The Year of Garrett and Melissa. I click the X to close the file, annoyed with myself.

A knock hits my door.

"Come in." I double-check my screen to make sure all evidence of my snooping is gone.

Sydney Shaw walks in. "Miss Rose?"

"Hi, Sydney. Come in."

She takes a seat in the chair in front of me. After staring at pictures of Melissa just a second ago, I see the resemblance to Sydney now. Most people in town think she's more Garrett than Melissa, but I think that's because Melissa isn't walking the streets side by side with her.

"Um...I was wondering." She looks out my window. Not much of a scene other than the parking lot. The other side gets the view of the ocean. "Do you think you'd be willing to take me to the store?"

"Oh. Of course." I stand to go to the nurse's station. "Did you need more pads?"

"No." She shakes her head. "I went last night."

I tilt my head and scrunch up my forehead because her dad was at the meeting until well after everything was closed.

"I rode my bike."

I nod. I don't know whether to feel sorry for Garrett or to slap him upside the head. This girl has no one and he's so confused on what to do that it seems he's doing nothing, which isn't helping matters.

"Would you like to go after school?" I ask her, sitting down on the chair next to her.

"Um...I need to go to the mall."

The mall is thirty miles away.

"Okay, I'd be happy to take you, but we'll have to tell your dad."

She rolls her eyes.

"Sydney, I can't take you without him knowing."

Her shoulders drop, but she nods. "Okay. Pick me up after school. I'll tell him." She stands from her chair.

"Sydney?" I call out before she clears my office door.

She turns around, her books in her hands.

"You still set with enough pads?"

Her cheeks redden and she nods. "Yes."

Then she's gone. Not one for small talk—well I sure know who she gets that from.

<hr>

At four o'clock, I pull into the Shaw's driveway. It's a log cabin up in the hills and not too far away from the rest of the cabins Garrett's built as rentals. The property they live in now was the first one he rented out for years before moving him and Sydney into it.

Garrett's truck is in the driveway and my stomach clenches with the thought of having to talk to him. My assumption is Sydney needs a bra and that's why she's coming to me. I didn't want to push her in my office because I'm sure it was hard enough to even ask me if I'd help her in the first place, without forcing her to explain why.

I've noticed a lot of the girls in her grade wearing them —mostly because the boys think they're funny and pull them, hoping they unhook.

Little assholes.

I ring the doorbell and hear his footsteps on the other side before the door swings open.

From his surprised look, he wasn't expecting me. "Charlie?" he asks, not moving from the door.

Sydney jogs down the stairs with her purse crossways on her body.

"I'm going shopping with Charlie. I'll be back later."

Garrett grabs ahold of her arm to stop her from escaping. "I'm sorry, what is going on?"

Sydney looks down, peeking up at me through her eyelashes.

"Sydney, why don't you meet me in the Jeep. Let me talk to your dad."

Garrett narrows his eyes at me but releases Sydney.

She rises up on her toes and kisses him on the cheek. "Thanks, Dad."

His eyes never leave me. "Don't thank me, I haven't said you can go yet."

She falls back on the heels of her feet and she sulks on her way to my car.

"May I?" I motion with my hand to the inside of the cabin.

He opens the door further and allows me in, shutting it behind me.

Caterpillars morph into butterflies in my stomach because I'm alone with Garrett Shaw in his house. This is where he sleeps, where he eats and right away my mind wanders to a vision of him in his underwear watching television. Which is absurd because he has a preteen daughter.

"Why are you taking my daughter shopping?" He pats his back pockets, then his front, obviously searching for something.

"She asked me and I'm guessing she doesn't want to ask you, so it must be personal."

"I'm her dad, what can't she ask me?"

I lean on the back of the brown leather couch, watching him flip cushions up and down and walk from the kitchen to the family room and back to the kitchen.

"I thought you got pretty good grades in school?" He stops his searching and stares at me. "I mean, you started this business from scratch so I'd think you were somewhat intelligent, Garrett. So, what gives?"

"What?" His forehead creases.

"Why do you act so dense when it comes to Sydney and the changes she's going through? Did you think she'd stay three forever?"

Maybe I'm being harsh, but someone has to make him see that puberty is in full force in the Shaw household. I mean adult diapers and a period party the other night? Give me a break, he's smarter than this.

"Did I miss you having a kid of your own?" He crosses his arms over that broad chest of his and if I didn't know we were about to go toe-to-toe I might drool.

"Don't play the whole I-don't-know-what-it's-like-because-I-don't-have-kids card."

"It's true. You have no idea how hard it is to know that my daughter doesn't need or want me anymore. You think I keep tabs on the latest feminine products? If it's as major to her as it is to me that she got her fucking period, then maybe she should have a party. Don't pretend to know what it's like to be a man raising a daughter on your own who is almost a teenager. I've got enough problems as it is right now and I don't need you giving me the gears about any of it."

"Okay." I hold my hands up in the air. "Let's start this over."

His hands still stay crossed over his broad chest.

"I refuse to be shut out of her life."

"Then I suggest you hop aboard the puberty train because it's not going to wait for you to be ready. She's growing up, Garrett."

He turns around, but I catch his hand move to his beard. A low grumble leaves his mouth.

"So, I'm going to take her to the mall now. I'll have her back after dinner if that's okay with you?"

He turns back around. "I'm coming with you."

"My Jeep isn't the train I was referring to," I deadpan.

"We'll take my truck," he says leaving no room for argument. He spots his phone on the kitchen counter and sighs in relief, then stuffs it in his pocket.

"I'm not sure she wants that."

He's already walking to the door, opening it.

"Well, either we go through this change together or not at all." He walks out the front door, waiting for me to join him.

"Technically, that's not true. The change is going to happen regardless—"

"Get in my truck, Charlie."

"I'm just saying, you have no control over it and I get that's hard for you—"

"Charlie," he sighs.

"Not to mention, she's not going through menopause."

He waves to Sydney who is nice and comfortable in the front of my Jeep.

She rolls her eyes and climbs out.

"What's going on?" she asks.

"Your dad is coming with us."

Garrett says nothing but climbs into the driver's side of his truck.

"I'm drawing the line on the changing room." Sydney shakes her head and climbs into the backseat of her dad's truck.

Is that supposed to mean I sit up front?

Shit, that's awkward.

Garrett honks the horn and I startle.

I open the passenger door and the scent of Garrett hits

my nostrils. It's a manly smell, woodsy almost, but hard to pinpoint. The only thing my body seems to know is that it's Garrett's smell because I inhale deeply and my stomach gets that tingling sensation it sometimes does when he's near.

"Maybe it should be your intelligence we're questioning," Garrett says, while I stand there. "I mean, you open the door and use the step to climb in."

My head turns in his direction. I expect to find his familiar scowl, but instead he's smiling.

"That's not nice, Dad," Sydney sticks up for me.

"I was deciding if I wanted to be this close to you or not," I say and hop up to take my seat.

He turns the key in the ignition and leans over really close to grab something from the glove box.

"We both know you do."

He grabs his sunglasses, places them over his eyes and pulls out of the driveway like he didn't just admit that he knows I've wanted him for years.

5

CHARLIE

Garrett parks his truck in the last fucking spot at the edge of the parking lot.

"Am I training for a marathon I don't know about?" I ask as the three of us bypass the row of empty parking spots on the way to the mall entrance.

"It's his new truck. We go through this for a few months." Sydney spins her index finger in a circle by her temple.

"Unless either of you want to pay to fix scratches and dents, I suggest you relax your jaws and keep your legs moving."

"I guess the exercise will do me good," I say and Garrett glances over, his eyes fixating on my chest.

"Oh Miss Rose, you don't need exercise," Sydney says.

I put my arm around her shoulders. "Aw, can I adopt you?"

Garrett takes a hold of her arm. "Sorry, she's not for sale."

Sydney stares up at him with a he's-my-savior look. She places her head on his chest and he kisses the top of her head. From the way Garrett's eyes close for a moment, I'd say this affection is rare.

Garrett opens the door to the mall for us and we file in.

"So, we'll meet you at the food court in about an hour?" I say to him when we reach the outside of the store.

Garrett looks at the mannequins all scantily clad in the display window. "Can I talk to you for a second?"

"Go in and look around Sydney, I'll be right there."

Once Sydney's in the store, looking at what it has to offer, Garrett sets his gaze on me.

"This is a little inappropriate, don't you think?"

I glance back at the store.

"No. Would you rather have me take her to the sports store and get her a sports bra?"

"Those are not bras for a twelve-year-old girl." He points to a picture of a model with a skimpy pink and black bra and panty set.

"No, they aren't."

"Then why are you taking her here? Those bras come with expectations. Expectations my twelve-year-old shouldn't know anything about."

I purse my lips together. "First of all, your daughter can't fill out one of those bras."

His gaze falls to my own breasts and a small part of me hopes he's envisioning me in that pink and black set.

"But there are other bras in there for her." I place my hand on his forearm. "Trust me. I won't let you down."

To my surprise he doesn't retract his arm, merely looks down at me and nods.

"I'm heading to one store and then I'll be in the food court." He digs into his back pocket and opens his wallet, handing me a credit card. "Here."

I take the card from him.

Without another word, his back is to me and he's walking away. His cargo pants are low on his hips and his long sleeve Henley is a little snugger than usual.

I might never be able to have him but a girl can still snap mental images for her finger vault can't she?

Shaking my head, I meet Sydney inside the store. She's looking at a pair of thong underwear.

"Yeah, no." I take it out of her hands and put it back on the rack. "Let's go to your section."

We end up in the teen area and I'm amazed at the selection. No more just white, tan, and cream cotton bras with a pink bow in the middle. This stuff is actually fun and fashionable.

"I'm loving these bralettes." I put one up to my chest. A chest that would most definitely be pouring out of one of these.

"They're all so cute, I can't decide," Sydney says from inside the fitting room.

"I love the mint green lace one that criss-crosses," I say, sitting down in the chair.

"Me too, but there's a rainbow striped one that looks like a unicorn that's awesome, too."

Sydney's usually been so quiet and reserved when I see her, but seeing this side of her is nice.

"Well, let's get four to start you off. So, get those and pick two others."

"Really? Oh great."

"It's on your dad, so no worries."

We both laugh.

My phone chimes with a text and I look down at it in my hand.

· · ·

GARRETT: *BUY SOMETHING FOR YOURSELF AS A THANK YOU FOR what you're doing.*

I smile, my thumbs typing out my response before I can think better of it.

Me: *You can pick it out if you'd like.*

I imagine his cheeks reddening and him running his hand along his beard. Was that pushing the envelope too far?

Garrett: *Send me a picture and I'll okay it.*

Apparently not. I smile to myself.

Me: *Would you prefer me to model it?*

The three dots appear and then disappear and reappear again.

I second-guess sending the cheeky text and quickly brush off my unease. What's a little flirting between friends? If you can even call us that…

"Syd, are you good?" I ask, still staring down at my phone as the three dots continue their disappearing act.

"Yeah, I have about six more to try on."

"Okay, I'm just going to look around the store."

"All right."

I head into the store, finding a black push up bra and see-through panties on display. Snapping a picture, I send it off to Garrett.

Again, the three dots appear and then disappear.

Garrett: *Whatever you like.*
Me: *I'm undecided on this set or...*

Before I can even take a picture, he responds.

Garrett: *No more pictures, just buy whatever.*

I snap the picture of a red lacy half cup demi bra and thongs panties.

Garrett: *Enough, Charlie.*
Me: *Maybe I should model them for you?*
Garrett: *Vance would kill me.*
Me: *Vance is in LA.*
Garrett: *Just buy both then.*
Me: *I don't want to spend all your money. I'm happy to have you be the decision maker.*
Garrett: *I have enough money, buy both.*

I laugh to myself and decide to head back to the dressing room to check on Sydney. On the way I see a pink bodysuit with a slit down the middle that reaches all the way down to the naval. It's lacy and see through. I snap a picture.

Me: *Maybe this would be more flattering on me?*
Garrett: *Jesus. How the hell am I going to hide this hard-on in the FOOD COURT?*
Me: *Is that a compliment?*
Garrett: *Take it however you want.*
Me: *I'll take it as a compliment. As long as it's me you're imagining in the lingerie and not someone else.*
Garrett: *You know exactly what I'm envisioning. Vance would string me up by my balls if he knew.*

Me: *Vance is in LA and I'm a grown woman, remember?*
Garrett: *I don't have to remember. I see your grown womanhood every damn day.*

"There you are," Syd says as she comes up alongside me.

"Oh." The phone drops from my hands and falls to the floor. "How did you do?" I bend down to pick it up.

"You okay?" Sydney's eyes widen. "Your face is flushed."

"I'm fine." I shove my phone in my back pocket and eye her items. Cute and preteenish. "Perfect, so you're all set?"

"Um...yeah." She's still eyeing me skeptically but seems to let the topic go.

"Let's go. Your dad is waiting for us."

Sydney glances at the bodysuit her dad and I were just discussing.

"Eyes forward." I snap my fingers in front of her face and her head turns in my direction.

"Um...okay," she says with a strange look on her face, but follows me to the register anyway.

"Chloe!" Sydney spots her friend Chloe, and bypasses her dad, to go right to her friend.

I sit down at the table with Garrett, tearing off a piece of his pretzel.

"Hey," he eyes me, but I dip it into his cheese sauce.

"Shopping is exhausting." I lean back in the chair.

"She got what she needed?" he asks.

"Yeah." I sit up straighter pulling his credit card out from my pocket. "Here you go." I slide it across the table.

"Thanks." He takes it and places it back in his wallet.

For some reason, that simple act—the way he leans to

the side and reaches in his back pocket, flicks open the wallet and slides the card in before putting it back in his pocket, is a complete turn on. The act is masculine and it's clear he's done it a million times before but something about it has me squeezing my thighs together.

"I don't see a bag in your hands?" He raises an eyebrow.

"You're giving mixed signals," I say it in a singsong voice, trying to keep this conversation light because more than anything I don't want to go back to being Charlie and Garrett who barely utter one word to each other.

"I might not date, Charlie, but I'm not blind and I am a red-blooded male. You think I haven't jerked off in twelve years?"

Great, now that image is floating around in my head and I'm really tingling between my legs. No amount of thigh clenching is going to help now.

I lean forward, folding my hands over one another. "Have you ever jerked off to me?"

He diverts his gaze.

"Something intriguing over at the pretzel stand?" I keep my own gaze locked on him.

"Vance told me to take care of you," he grinds out between clenched teeth.

"So you do want something forbidden?" A laugh is floating up my throat. The fact that I'm having this entire conversation with him is as surprising as Dane finding a woman who can tolerate him. But I guess miracles happen every day.

"Here." He places a bag on the table. "As a thank you for helping me with Sydney."

He's dodging the question and I can tell that if I push any further he's going to completely shut down on me. I'll let it go for now, but we *will* be revisiting this conversation.

I open the bag to find a name plaque for my desk.

"It's not much, but I noticed Mrs. Quentin's was still on your desk when I was there the other day."

I pull out the silver-plated rectangle engraved with the words Charlotte Rose.

My heart warms and my cheeks rise with a wide smile.

"Thank you. But you didn't need to do this. I'm happy to help anytime." I place it back in the bag.

He slides the pretzel my way after I pull off another bite. Looking over his shoulder to make sure Sydney is talking to Chloe, the mood at the table becomes melancholy.

"After Melissa died, I thought I had years before this happened. She needs a mom figure to talk to."

"I'm here for her at school and out of school. We're friends Garrett, I've known you my entire life." I pop another piece of pretzel in my mouth. That salad from lunch did not do its job of filling me up.

"She's going to leave me soon. Have her own life. Sometimes I wonder if I made a mistake by not remarrying."

Is he really having a heart to heart with me?

"Well, she was your true love. Your soul mate. I imagine that's hard to replace."

He huffs and looks at me. "Can you really say that about someone that you faced no challenges with? Sometimes I wonder if we'd have stayed together while we raised Charlie."

"Oh, I'm sure you would have."

"I'm glad you think so. We were so young when we married. Neither one of us had ever been with anyone else. Maybe she would have gotten sick of Climax Cove. There are a million scenarios and things that could've gone wrong."

I reach over and place my hand on his. Surprisingly, he doesn't move it away.

"I wouldn't waste your time thinking about what ifs."

"Isn't that what life is all about, the what ifs?" he asks and I remove my hand from on top of his.

"Then I think you're not living your life to the fullest." I dip another piece of pretzel into the cheese and eat it.

Garrett looks behind him at Sydney and then back to me.

"When did Little Charlie Rose become so smart?" He smiles showing he's playing with me.

"When she grew tits and an ass."

He laughs and shakes his head like he usually does when I talk. "And mighty fine tits and ass they are."

Now, it's my cheeks flushing. I swear I should look around the food court. I've got to be on candid camera.

6

GARRETT

It's been a few days since the whole period thing with Sydney. I haven't asked any questions and she hasn't offered any information either. Instead of the period party the guys thought was such a great idea, I opted for a celebration dinner of our own without truly announcing it.

"I'll be right back." I park the truck outside Happy Daze Tavern.

"I'm starving," Syd whines, but I shut the truck door and hurry in to drop off the cabin key to Dane.

My stomach does some twisty bullshit thing when my hand lands on the handle of the door, but I shake it off and enter the bar. There are only a few groups milling around, some playing darts and a few regulars lining the bar.

On instinct my gaze lands behind the bar and that feeling in my stomach vanishes when I spot Chad, Dane's other employee serving drinks. He nods at me and I do the same, sliding between the tables to the back office.

My knuckles hit the wood door and my hand moves to the doorknob. It's locked.

"Dane!" I say, and a loud crashing sound comes from within.

"Shit," I hear from behind the door followed by a bunch of scrambling.

I'm not in the mood to catch a glimpse of Dane's groin cleavage he's so proud of.

"Here." I slide the envelope under the door.

His laughing and Ava's giggling commence and I assume they're either still getting it on or trying to get dressed.

I walk back down the hallway shaking my head to myself. I'm not gonna lie, the amount of sex they have forces me to remember the good times in a relationship—the sex whenever and wherever you want part. That thought is immediately followed by the vision of a certain chestnut-haired girl. Her curls spread out on my pillow and her ample tits in my hands.

Fuck, what am I doing?

Vance, I forcibly remind myself. Your best friend who you promised you'd take care of his baby sister? Plus, there's no way Charlie could be my guinea pig even if I was ready to give a relationship a try.

I head out of the tavern and climb back into the cab of my truck, finding Syd on her phone. No surprise there.

"Okay, let's go." I crank the ignition and a text message dings on my phone.

"What was that about?" she asks, which surprises me because lately my errands are only a thorn in her side and she never much cares what I'm doing, just more when I'll be done.

"I had to drop off a key to one of the cabins."

I fiddle with the radio to turn it off her station and back onto my classic rock. She groans and I let my smile shine on the inside. Isn't it a father's responsibility to make his preteen daughter's life unbearable?

"Dane and Ava are renting a cabin?"

Shocked by her talkative mood, I turn to give her my attention. "No, Charlie, um...Miss Rose."

"Dad. She's been Charlie my entire life."

"Well, at school she's Miss Rose."

"I'm aware." There's the tone that's been missing this outing. The tone that suggests she has no idea how I made it this far in life because I am a complete moron.

"Watch your tone, Sydney."

She ignores my attempt at discipline. "You letting Charlie stay in a cabin?"

I raise both eyebrows. "She bid on it, remember?"

"I also remember you pulling her into the hallway."

Fuck, sometimes I forget how observant she can be. Especially when she barely talks to me, it's easy to forget she doesn't miss much.

"I was worried she didn't have the money."

She looks out the window and I move the gearshift to put the truck into drive.

"You're letting her stay for free?" Now it's her eyebrows shooting up to her hairline. "Interesting."

"What?"

"Just you and Miss Rose. That's all."

I glance to the side to see her shrug.

"Now she's Miss Rose?"

"I want to respect my elders, especially if she might be my stepmom one day."

My foot slips off the brake and I slam it back down before running into Dane's Jeep.

"Tell me Syd, does getting your period, make you think crazy thoughts?"

She giggles. "You like her."

"No, I don't."

"Yes, you do."

"No. I. Don't."

"Who sounds like the adolescent now?" She begins to type away on her phone again with that know it all smirk.

"She's Vance's little sister. I've practically known her since she was born."

"Whatever you say, Dad."

My foot eases off the brake and I start pulling into traffic when my phone dings with another text message. I throw the truck into park with a growl, flustered and annoyed.

Dane: *Thanks, buddy.*
Dane: *I'll make sure she gets the key and I'll happily pay the grand for it since I know I don't pay her enough to afford it. :P*

Sitting in the truck, I type out my response quickly.

Me: *It's fine. I've already paid it. She's been doing me a solid with Syd lately and deserves it.*
Dane: *Hmm ... if I didn't know better ...*
Me: *Just go back to fucking your girlfriend.*
Dane: *Remember that lecture you gave me? I'm reaping the rewards lately. You should take your own advice.*
Me: *Stock up. Droughts happen.*
Dane: *Not when you're Dane Murray.*

"I'm starving, Dad," Syd whines again.

"Okay, okay." I place my phone in the cup holder, putting the truck in gear.

We head out of town toward Wet Rock and Sydney glances over to me once she figures out where we're headed.

"Dinner with Nana and Papa?" There's a note of disappointment in her voice.

Nana and Papa are Melissa's parents who recently moved thirty miles outside of Climax Cove. They could very well be my own set of parents. After Melissa died, I think caring for Sydney helped them through the grieving process. I'm sad to say it took me longer and every time I held Syd, I thought about Melissa, which in turn made me depressed. It was an ugly cycle that I'm thankful has stopped.

"Nana keeps asking me to help her with her phone."

"She's seventy, Syd. Give her a break." We make the drive to my in-laws, which have become few and far between as of late.

"I see Grandma all the time on Instagram."

I glance to my side. "I think she sees it as a way to keep in touch with you."

"She friended Chloe the other day."

I shake my head, smiling to myself because Chloe is Syd's crazy friend. Everyone has that one friend who comes into your house, helps themselves to anything in the fridge and makes themselves at home. The one who always plops down on your couch after a long ass day, only wanting to drink a beer and watch a game. Chloe is to Syd, what Dane is to me.

"Chloe pressed the decline button right?"

She raises her eyebrows with a smirk. "What do you think?"

"And?"

Her giddy laugh reminds me of simpler times between us.

"And Chloe started asking her how bummed she was about One Direction breaking up."

"What did Nana say?"

Another giggle escapes and bounces around the cab of the truck. I can't help the smile that's on my face.

"She said they'll catch up to one another if they're all going in the same direction."

Sydney bends over in a fit of laughter, spurring my own amusement from my daughter's reaction.

"Well, just be happy she's not on SnapChat."

"Can you imagine? It'd be her and Papa figuring out the camera for the whole ten seconds."

"They could be a YouTube sensation." I take a second to glance over at her.

She slaps her leg and again bends over, laughing.

My heart warms from our ability to fill the thirty-minute drive with more than silence and whatever station she wants to listen to on the radio. I, for one, was thankful when One Direction broke up.

By the time we're pulling into Nana and Papa's driveway, I'm hopeful that there's a possibility I'll get through these teenage years unscathed.

"Oh. My. God. Dad, look at the goose." Sydney's covering her face with her hands and shaking her head back and forth.

We both stare at the front porch where a goose sculpture is dressed up like a turkey in honor of Thanksgiving in a few weeks.

"Just be happy your Nana didn't put that on Instagram," I say and my little girl laughs. I soak in the sound while I can.

At the dinner table, Violet, Sydney's Nana, keeps eyeing me as she places dishes down on the table. Phil is busy with his crossword puzzle, asking Syd the answers. He thinks his granddaughter is a genius.

"You should get her tested. She's gifted." He barely peeks up from the paper, asking her another question. "All right Syd, Cube creator Rubik?"

"That box thing with all the different colors?" Violet asks placing some bread on the table. "I remember Melissa changing the stickers, pretending she finished it." Her smile falters for a second and even after twelve years, everyone in this room can feel how much she misses her daughter.

Syd's thumbs move across the screen of her phone. "Erno," she says.

"That's it. You're amazing." Papa tosses her another accolade.

Sydney smiles down at her phone and then eyes me as I pick up my fork and dig in.

"Oh, Sydney, after dinner, can you help me with my phone?" Violet asks as she takes a seat. "I tried to use that Google Map thing the other day and I don't understand it. Bea said that it's supposed to be easier than MapQuest."

"What's MapQuest?" Sydney asks.

"Look, Phil, I know something she doesn't." Violet nudges her husband's arm with her own.

"Because it was around before she was born."

Violet's crystal blue eyes stare at him until he looks over the rim of his reading glasses. "I used it to get you to the hospital the other day just fine." She cocks her hip to the side.

He shakes his head.

"What?" Sydney places her phone on the table and looks between the two of them.

I place my fork on the plate and wipe my mouth.

"Are you okay, Phil?" I ask.

He shakes his head. "I'm fine." He shoots Violet a look and it's clear he's not happy that she said anything.

"Just heartburn," Violet says, rising from the table.

Sydney looks to me and I smile a reassuring grin to calm her worries that probably match my own.

"So, you're good?" Sydney asks her papa.

He smiles and nods. "Perfect. I'm a Marine after all. Gonna take a lot to keep this ol' guy down." His eyes focus on the paper in front of him. "Now, my genius of a granddaughter, what's the Spanish word for attract through one's charm?"

Sydney's thumbs move across her screen.

Violet walks back in with a stack of napkins.

"Second to last letter is a d," he continues.

"Put the paper away, Phil." Violet's voice has an edge now.

"Duende," Sydney answers.

He presses the pen to the paper and then takes off his glasses, setting them on top of the paper. "Seriously, Garrett, you need to get her tested."

"I think hacking might be more her thing." I eye Syd and she smirks.

"Dad, you are duending Miss Rose."

"I don't think I'll be scheduling that test anytime soon." I direct my attention to Sydney. "Wouldn't it be used like, Miss Rose is duende?"

"I don't think that's right either. Do you know how to find the answer on that phone?" Phil asks Sydney and she smiles and nods.

Violet holds up her hand. "Regardless of how to use it, it means attractive. Who is Miss Rose?" Her gaze volleys between Sydney and me.

I cock my jaw. "It's Charlotte Rose. You know...Vance Rose's little sister."

"And the new counselor at my school," Sydney adds.

"And you like her?" Violet asks.

"No."

"Yes," Sydney counters.

"No."

"Yep," she says.

I shoot Sydney a look that says quit it and she giggles.

"You do." Violet points to me. "Your cheeks are pink."

I roll my eyes. "She's been helping me out the last week or so."

"How so?"

Sydney's giant smile drops and her eyes widen. Now it's my turn to embarrass her. Tell her grandparents how she's got her period and a bra all in one week.

"Just some stuff with Syd's classes and things."

"Oh." Violet picks up her fork.

"Well, you know it's about time you find someone." She looks over to Phil whose fork is pushing around his stroganoff on his plate. "I mean, we *want* you to find someone."

The mood at the table shifts and the light-hearted humor from minutes before has disappeared. Sydney buries her head back in her phone.

"Right, Syd?" Violet doesn't let the topic go. "You want your dad to be happy..."

Sydney glances over to me and then back to her phone with a shrug. "Yeah."

"See, Garrett." Violet's hand covers mine. "If Charlie is

the one you want, you should go for it. Don't let Phil and I stop you."

I could ramble about ten different reasons and none of them are Violet and Phil, although it *would* be awkward to bring a woman here ever.

"I'm not ready."

Sydney's chair slides across the floor. We all look and she's standing. "I have to go to the bathroom. Don't read into things." She disappears down the hall and the bathroom door shuts a minute later.

"Don't worry. She'll be fine when you are ready."

Phil places his glasses back on and picks up his pen. Violet begins eating again and I sit there wondering how Syd really would be if I was ever ready.

She never even knew Melissa.

I don't have time to give it any more thought because my phone dings in my pocket. I pull it out to find a text from Charlie.

Charlie: *How do I work this hot tub?*

Christ do I ever wish I *was* ready right now.

7

CHARLIE

Freezing my ass off in my white bikini wasn't exactly what I envisioned when I imagined myself spending a quiet night in one of Garrett's cabins, away from my roommates. With Marcus constructing a studio for Cat, they've been staying at our apartment with Lily. One day, I'll be the only one in that apartment. Cat will eventually move in with Marcus and Ava with Dane, but for now, they're paying rent for a room neither of them usually sleep in. Exactly why Ava didn't mind giving up her room for Lily when Cat said they needed somewhere to stay for awhile.

Not only do I have the weekend off from Happy Daze, but I have the entire log cabin to myself. My wine glass sits on the counter, lonely without the bubbles of the hot tub surrounding it. Walking over to the counter, I gulp it down, as I wait for Garrett's maintenance guy to get out here.

Garrett Shaw. Him complimenting my tits and ass the other day still replays in my head. Sadly, it was probably the highlight of my year, besides landing my full-time gig at the school. That night at the mall was the old Garrett—captain of the rugby team, prankster who might have filled your locker with popcorn, but would have your back whenever you needed him.

The happy Garrett of yesteryear makes me remember the devastated one. The one I thought was never going to be functional again. I'm not even sure exactly when it happened, but it was a good few years before he really started putting his life back in order again. Still, that one night in my parents' basement always ignites those butterflies in my stomach.

It was a graduation party for me, I'd just finished high school and my parents threw me an eighteenth birthday party and graduation party at the same time.

My brother, Vance, returned from Los Angeles for it, so I'm not sure who the party was really for, me or him.

Garrett had shown up, and that's when I first saw him with a beard. My nipples peaked and I clenched my thighs together.

"God, he's bigger than high school," my friend, Bree, said from next to me.

We both stared at him as he strolled in with Sydney's hand in his.

"She's the spitting image of him except she's got those gorgeous big blue eyes," Bree carried on and I would have responded if my mouth wasn't suddenly drier than Deb's chicken down at Double D's.

Garrett was in a pair of board shorts and a T-shirt with soccer slides on. There were a few of Melissa's friends there and they immediately circled Sydney who was clinging to her daddy's leg.

He picked her up and she seemed to fit so perfect in his strong arms. She pushed her head into the crook of his neck. Garrett tried to get Sydney to engage with the girls who were fawning all over her, repeating telling her how beautiful she was. No one mentioned what Bree had, that her eyes were Melissa's eyes because after she died, no one ever said her name unless it was a whisper and never to Garrett.

Then, Jane, Garrett's mom came over.

All she had to do was hold her arms out and Sydney left Garrett for her grandma. She carried her over to a table with my mom and a few others. They all cooed over her and Jane fed her.

My vision shifted from Sydney to Garrett who was now surrounded by women.

Vance and their other high school friends came over and they all hung around the loungers by the pool. The girls flaunting their chests, the boys took off their shirts, showing how much more muscle they'd developed since high school.

"Your brother's friends are so hot," Bree whispered in my ear.

I sip the beer I snuck from the keg out of my red solo cup. Sitting down, I tried to concentrate on my friends, even Dylan, my prom date. We weren't official or anything but I knew he wanted to be a couple. But he was leaving on scholarship in the fall and I wasn't into a summer fling followed by a long distance relationship.

My eyes kept betraying me. They kept seeking Garrett out, wanting to know what he was doing.

Then I was on my way to the bathroom and a group of my friends were joking around and pushed me into the pool. My solo cup went flying, my body sunk into the cold water. I kind of wanted to stay down there a little longer in the silence, but two hands reached under my arms and pulled me from the water.

I surfaced and blinked, finding Garrett's gruff face in front of mine.

"You okay?" he asked and my head went fuzzy and light.

I nodded. "Thanks," I managed to say.

To this day, I can remember the feel of his abs as my fingers brushed against him while I gained some stability. The smell of him. Not cologne, but just this manly scent that is Garrett. At that point in my life, he still intimidated me—big, gruff, standoffish Garrett. But in that moment, Melissa triggered in my mind. Mostly, it was his eyes...kind and gentle. That was the side she saw.

It made me wonder how he took her virginity. Was he gentle when he glided in that first time? I was envious of Melissa right then because I'd opted to give my virginity to Dylan who didn't take care with me at all.

"Better lay off the keg for awhile," he suggested and pulled away to go back to his water volleyball game. He picked up the beach ball and hit it over the net.

Dylan was standing at the ladder as I climbed up, his eyes pointed to Garrett's back.

"So, is that why you won't give me the time of day? You want Shaw?"

He said it louder than I'd prefer since a few heads turned in my direction.

"No," I mumbled, heading toward the house since a change of clothes was now in order thanks to my friends.

"Get real, Charlie. He doesn't see you."

Again with the loud voice.

I stopped, turned, and stomped over to him.

"Shut up," I whisper yelled. It's then I smelled the alcohol on his breath. I knew some of the guys had brought flasks but hadn't realized that Dylan had had that much to drink.

"Shut up? Don't talk to me like that. Garrett Shaw sees you as one thing only, his best friend's little sister." His eyes dipped down my body. "He'd never want you. Melissa was the complete opposite of you. She was thin and super girly and you're, well, not."

My face heated as the crowd grew around us, their gazes feeling like a spotlight on a stage.

"Dylan, you're a fucking asshole. Get out." I threw my arm out, pointing to the back gate of my parents' fence.

He laughed. "I can't believe I wasted my time on you. Garrett Shaw. That's my competition? You're clueless, Charlie. Fucking clueless."

He started walking at the persistence of some of his friends that had gathered near. Bree found her way over to me, sheltering my now tear stricken face in her embrace.

"There a problem?"

I turned from Bree to see that Vance was up and out of the pool, water dripping off his body as he walked over to us.

His chestnut hair that matched my own making him look like a model out of a perfume ad. Seriously, Dylan was right. I was curvy and looked nothing like Melissa. My brother somehow got the chiseled jaw, soft brown eyes, and the curl of his hair was wavier than my uncontrolled spirals. Many times I wondered how he won the genetic lottery, every great feature of my mom and dad bestowed on him and all I got was the leftovers.

"Your sister's a fucking tease." Dylan threw the comment over his shoulder and I knew it was the alcohol that had given him the courage.

"What did you say?" Vance stomped over to Dylan and his friends.

"He's drunk, Rose," someone called out.

"Let it be, Vance," another said.

My brother looked at me and then to the pool, but he didn't have to call to his friends. Garrett and the three others still here were already climbing out.

Thank God all the real adults are in the house.

"No. Don't." I left Bree to stand in between the two of them.

Dylan's chest pressed against my open palm.

"What are you gonna do, Rose? Hit me. I'm seventeen. Good luck with that." The cockiness in Dylan's voice had me wanting to clock him.

"You think my uncle is going to throw me in jail?" Vance baited him. "Who's fucking clueless now?"

The weight of their chests was crushing my arms. Vance never once looked down at me, keeping his narrowed gaze on Dylan.

"Stop fucking with my sister."

"You mean stop fucking her?" Dylan smirked and his intention of throwing Vance off his game was effective.

Vance's gaze shot down to my own. "Please say no."

I saw the pleading look in his eyes and shifted my gaze to Garrett who was next to Vance. There were those soft eyes once more. He bit his lip.

Vance took me and shoved me to the side. "You fucking asshole."

Then Dylan was on the ground, Vance standing over him and I somehow stumbled into Garrett's arms again, staring into those eyes.

"Stay the fuck away from her!" Vance yelled.

"I think you should look next to you, she's moved onto Shaw now."

God, this idiot didn't know when to quit.

Garrett's gaze shifted to my brother and he righted me. I wobbled as I tried to find my footing after feeling so secure.

"What the fuck man? She's your little sister," Garrett scoffed. "Come on, we're winning." He ran and jumped in the pool and I swear I felt as cold as that water.

"Do me a favor? Don't screw anymore assholes." Vance followed Garrett and then all eyes seemed to turn away from me.

Dylan got up off the ground and cursed under his breath as he and his friends left.

Later that night, after everyone had gone home, I headed to the basement. I couldn't sleep after everything that happened so I thought I'd watch some television, but when I reached the bottom of the stairs and turned on the light, Garrett was sitting on our couch, his phone in his hands.

"Hey," he looked over at me and then tucked his phone in his pocket.

"I'm sorry. I didn't know you stayed." I shifted my body to head back upstairs.

"Wait. You don't have to go." I turned to face him but stayed where I was, keeping a safe distance between us. "My mom took Syd so I stayed the night here after drinking."

I nodded, rocking back on my heels. His eyes roamed up and down my body, but there was no sign of lust, just indifference. I mentally high-fived myself for wearing boxer shorts and a camisole. My breasts were practically hanging out. Maybe he'd like what he saw and wouldn't think of me as Vance's little sister anymore.

"You really screwed that douche?" he asked.

I walked toward the couch, but stayed behind it, my hands clenching the top of the cushion.

"Yeah."

"Dylan Scott is an asswipe. Don't listen to him."

I didn't know what he meant by that. Everyone at the party clearly heard him saying I was after Garrett.

"Yeah, I should have thought twice about him."

"You can do a lot better." The way he said it, like he was sincere and really believed it, like they weren't just trite words he was throwing out there, only intensified my want of him.

I nodded my head slowly.

"Guys are so immature at your age." He shook his head in disgust.

My head seemed to involuntarily move up and down.

"I was such a loser."

I round the couch and sit down a seat cushion away from him. "You were great to Melissa at that age."

His head flew up so fast, his eyes searching for something, I didn't know what.

"I'm going to give you some advice. Things aren't always the same once you're in your own house."

I never understood what he meant when he said that.

"From what I saw, you treated her nice."

He shrugged, his big shoulders looking so broad.

"I'm not sure I'll ever find out the kind of man I would've become with the right woman."

I peeked over at him from the corner of my eye, my thighs pressed tightly together, hoping they didn't look too fat. "You'll find someone."

He shook his head. "No, I'm done in that department now."

It was like a vault door had been shut and locked. He's the rare jewel that sits locked away from everyone. No one would see the beauty of him, no one would know his value, no one would ever possess him again. He sealed himself closed and that's when I knew that Garrett Shaw would be the forever bachelor. Not because he was raising a daughter on his own and not because no one would ever compare to the woman he lost. I always knew it was fear that made that decision for him.

The doorbell rings and I shake my head and re-join the here and now. Placing my empty wine glass down, I tread across the hardwood floors, grabbing a towel to wrap around my waist.

Prepared for the pool man, I open the door, but my voice lodges in my throat.

There stands Garrett Shaw.

8

Snap a picture and caption it 'Teenage boy in front of his first Playboy' because that's exactly how I feel right now and I'd bet that's how I look.

Charlie stands in the doorway wearing a white bikini, her nipples hard and erect, begging to be touched. The first thing I notice is the way she doesn't cover up, but opens the door wider, ushering me in with her free hand.

"I expected the pool guy." Her voice changes pitch and I gather she's as affected by this situation as I am. The only difference is, my arousal can't be hidden.

"He's out of town, so you got me."

"And you can fix it?"

I stop and tilt my head her way. "Is that even a question?"

"Well," she walks faster to catch up to me as I use a key to open up the one door that's locked from guests. "Oh, I always wonder what's behind these doors when I rent other people's vacation homes." She peeks her head over my shoulder and the scent of her perfume makes a beeline for my dick, making it twitch.

As he's begging for an introduction, I squat to get away, but she doesn't relent. Her tits are practically resting on my shoulder.

"Ever heard of personal space?" I remark, grabbing my tool set.

"This isn't half as exciting as I thought it would be." She finally moves back and I stand with the toolbox in my hands.

"Did you think there would be a dead body?"

She shrugs. "Porn maybe?"

"Why would there be porn?"

She purses her lips and looks up at the ceiling. It's innocent and cute and I'm not sure I ever remember seeing her doing it before. "You know, the owner can't keep it in their own house because they have a preteen daughter, so they keep their stash in the closet and watch it when there are no guests here."

"Let me guess? I'm the guy with the preteen daughter."

"You're so smart. I see where Sydney gets it from." She smiles, a mouthful of straight white teeth.

I nod and walk away. She follows.

"Do you need help?"

"Since I really have no idea what I'm fixing, I don't know yet." I open the screen door to the hot tub.

"It wouldn't turn on."

"That's not a good sign."

I open up the back and start working on it. The little I know about hot tubs might not be enough.

Charlie sits on the edge of the hot tub and puts her feet in, her purple polished toenails dipping in and out of the water.

"I think I deserve a discount if I can't use the hot tub."

I look up at her and she's smirking.

"Funny."

She's quiet for a few minutes while I fiddle around trying to figure out the source of the problem.

"I'm curious, Garrett..." she pauses and I glance up at her. "How do my tits look in this bikini?"

At first, her words throw me. My mouth dries up and I have no retort back. Not that I was ever like Dane in that department. He and Charlie can spar back and forth all day.

"Do you need a self-esteem pick me up?"

"If I went by eye vision alone, I'd say you've already envisioned your mouth around my nipple." She places her hands back, her tits pressing out.

Fuck. Why is she making doing the right thing so goddamn difficult?

"I think you should remember I'm your brother's best friend." I try to concentrate on the small motor in front of me, but she's right, I want to rip the skimpy white material away from her body.

"Is he really your best friend anymore? He hasn't been around for years. Barely home for holidays. You haven't gone to visit him either. So, I'm not sure that's a justified strike against me."

My gaze travels up and quickly back down, but I saw enough to know her chest is heaving for a breath while she looks on at me.

"How about you're too young?"

"Yeah, that doesn't work either. I mean, you're thirty-four, I'm twenty-six, it's eight years. We're not talking Anna Nicole Smith here."

I shrug, grabbing my wrench.

"What about the fact that I've known you my entire life?"

"All the better. Our moms are friends. We both love Climax Cove. It's a win-win."

I blow out a breath. "Charlie, what exactly are you doing here?" I lean back and sit on my heels.

"You're the one who made the remark about my tits and ass at the mall."

"Yeah, and I shouldn't have." My grip tightens on the wrench.

"Don't you ever think once we get each other out of our system, we'll be good? That the attraction between us will diminish?"

I shake my head. "No."

"Yes, you do. I see it, Garrett, in the last few weeks, you've finally noticed me."

I stand up, moving over to the box on the wall. "Forget the school girl crush you have on me. It's not going to happen."

"See? You didn't deny you notice me and you admitted you knew about my crush."

"The entire town knows about the crush you have on me, but I told you in your basement that night, I'm done with relationships." I press the hot tub button and it turns on.

Thank God, I can get out of here before things get too out of control.

"I'm not asking for a relationship." She stands and opens the towel and I swallow the lump in my throat at the sight of her white bikini bottoms. "I know you couldn't have been celibate all these years."

"You want me to tell you the last time I was with a woman? Want me to tell you how I took her back to her hotel room and bent her over the dresser? Do you want all the details, Charlie, so you can remember them? Maybe envision yourself?"

I walk through the screen door, heading straight for the closet.

I need to get out of here.

"Well, at least then I'd know how I should be imagining you."

"You have some sort of fascination with me," I say, never turning around, but I hear her footsteps following.

"It's not a fascination." Her usual self-confident voice breaks. "This is your last opportunity, Garrett Shaw. Either you fuck me tonight or never."

I drop the toolbox in the closet and turn around.

"You only want me because you think I'm someone I'm not. You think I'm going to lay you down in that bed and make love to you. But I don't do that anymore, Charlie. I fuck. Plain and simple. There are no emotions involved and I leave never thinking of the woman again."

"Then fuck me."

"I can't." I lock up the door, my hand trembling on the doorknob.

"Why?" Her voice is losing the fight. "Is it because you're not attracted to me? Am I just too ugly and fat?" The tremor in her voice does me in.

I face her, only to see that while her voice might be broken, her eyes are screaming anger. I'm not even sure if I approached her if she'd kiss me or hit me and I'm not about to find out.

"You're gorgeous. And yes you're right...my mouth is watering thinking about sucking on your tits. My dick has been hard since you opened the door. And after you took off the towel, I wanted to find out whether you're bare or have a small patch. But fuck, Charlie, you're Vance's sister. There's no fucking you and leaving you tomorrow. I won't do it to you."

She steps up and I don't falter.

"I'm not that eighteen-year-old girl anymore. I'm not the scorned girl who was just embarrassed in front of a party. I'm twenty-six and I'm fully capable of fucking you for one reason and one reason only—to get you out of my system. Then this whole spark between us can be extinguished and forgotten about."

She doesn't get any closer but stays six inches away. She wants me to make the final move.

"Fine, have it your way." She swivels on her heels and saunters away.

One split second is all it takes for me to spin her back into my arms. Her body hits me with a humph and her brown eyes look up at me. God, I want to taste her. I want to lick her, I want to fuck her.

"What do you want Garrett?" she asks, breathless, her body tight against mine. Her tits are pressed against my chest and I can feel the hardened peaks of her pebbled nipples.

"Fuck." I use one hand to pull the ponytail from her hair and the long strands of curls flow over her shoulders. "I want to fuck you."

"I'm not going to stay wet forever," she says with a grin.

My mouth crashes down on hers. Our tongues fight for dominance and I win when I plant my two hands on either side of her face.

She tastes like red wine and I want to pour a bottle over her naked body and lick every drop off.

Her moan is what finally has me backing us up to the couch. I swallow down her sounds, my cock straining against my zipper.

Closing the kiss, my lips move down her jaw to her

throat as my fingers hook on either side of her bottoms, pushing them off her body.

"How could you think I didn't want you?" I mumble against her heated flesh but I know she understands me because her hands tighten in my hair.

"I want to feel you between my thighs," she says, propping herself up on the edge of the couch.

I'll never look at this brown leather piece of furniture the same again.

Pulling the fabric down her legs, I fling it over my shoulder then nudge her legs open. A small patch of neatly trimmed hair sits over top of her pussy. I hate clean-shaven. A woman should look like a woman as far as I'm concerned.

"You're fucking perfect." I swipe my finger along her slit and she wasn't lying, she's slick.

"Please, I need you." She takes my head and pulls it down to her lips.

Frantic and crazy, we kiss like we're starved. It's been a long time since I wanted something this much.

She pulls my lips off her and nudges my head lower.

We both know what she wants, and she'll get it, but not until I play with her chest first.

I've dreamed of feeling the weight of her tits in my hands. To know if her nipples are pink or brown.

I reach behind her back, untie the bikini top and it falls down, her tits bouncing into place. I was right when I said she was perfect. There, on both her breasts, lay perfectly round silver dollar nipples.

"I need to fuck these before the night is over."

My thumbs run over her nipples and she moans.

"Tell me you're a tit man..." she says half breathless.

"I'm an everything man when it comes to you, but I love a great set of tits."

I lean forward and take a nipple between my lips, circling it with my tongue and sucking until I release it from my mouth with a pop.

"And you, Charlotte Rose, have a great set of tits. One might even say perfect."

Once again, she pulls my face to hers and we kiss in an uncontrolled frenzy. Our tongues continue to glide and slide along one another's. I want the kiss to go on forever until. That is until I'm distracted by her hand reaching into my pants. She starts to unbutton and unzip my pants.

She bites down on her plump bottom lip. "You've seen me. Now it's my turn."

Charlie stands and her top falls to the hardwood floor, joining the bottom of the bikini.

Pulling my pants down, she reveals my boxers, the head of my dick sticking out.

"I knew he wanted to meet me." She stares up at me between my legs with my cock right at her mouth. Pulling it out, she licks the underside. "I see you're just as big as the rest of him. I've been wanting to meet you for a while." She's talking directly to my dick.

"Quit talking to my cock."

Her eyes are filled with lust as she strokes me up and down, her thumb rubbing the pre-cum around the tip.

"I'm just letting him know he's admired." She smiles and the sight of her looking up at me with my dick in her hands is almost unbearable.

All the times I've thought about being with her, this scenario never came up. Me bending her over a couch, or her riding me were pretty active in my imagination, I'm not going to lie. I may have imagined playing with her more-than-a-handful tits on numerous occasions.

"May I lick you?" she asks and I place my hands on each

side of her head, directing her to my dick.

"Charlie, no talking to the D."

She giggles while taking me into her mouth and shaking her head. Her mouth keeps moving down and she deep throats me, making me buck my hips.

"Shit." My fists tighten around her curls.

My dick pops out of her mouth and she looks up to me. "Are you still going to complain about me talking to Big G?"

I remove one hand from her hair and rub my thumb along her wet bottom lip.

"You can talk to him anytime you want. Now, don't forget to swallow."

I ease my cock back into her mouth and her fist clenches over the base, stroking me while she sucks.

I could make excuses at this point. I could say that her blow job skills are off the hook or say it's because I haven't been blown in years. When I've had sex, it's sex. Fucking actually and then it's over. I don't go down on the woman and she doesn't go down on me. It's more of a need to douse the sexual energy my hand can't control.

But with Charlie, the need is too great—the urge to have her wiggling against my tongue, my dick plunging into her from in front and behind. To watch her tits jiggle as she rides me. I'm not sure one night will get her out of my system.

Knowing time is not on our side, I'm not about to waste my load on a blow job right now. So, I regretfully pull my hips back and move her head from the end of my dick.

"Allow me to return the favor," I say.

Her eyes twinkle in that *please do* fashion.

"Are you going to talk to my pussy?" she asks, her voice that high-pitched sweet as sugar one she rarely uses.

"Don't worry. My tongue will do all the talking."

9

CHARLIE

I had worried that Garrett would be rusty. Not that I'm naïve enough to think that he's been celibate for twelve years, but I've never seen him with a woman, so I assume it's a fuck 'n chuck scenario.

Regardless, the man has the tongue of a magician. I keep waiting for him to peek his head out from between my legs to lay on top of me, but that hasn't happened yet. Instead, his beard scratches the inside of my thighs in the most arousing way.

My hands reach down and my fingers thread through the longer strands of hair on the top of his head as my back arches. A low deep growl sounds from him only drenching me further.

"Don't stop," I plead.

He shakes his head and his fingers dig into my hips as he pushes his face further into my center.

A tremble ignites and I wiggle my hips to extinguish that cusp my body is demanding. I don't want to come yet. I want to enjoy him down there. What I've imagined for years has finally come true like my own fairy godmother struck her wand and granted me a wish.

As much as I want to prolong this, Garrett's masterful tongue isn't giving me any choice.

"I'm going to come." My body twists and turns until he plants his hands on my stomach to keep me in place.

That growl murmurs into me once more and his tongue slides and sucks. Once he reaches up and squeezes both my nipples, I combust, unable to keep my orgasm at bay.

"Fuck!" I scream, the upper half of my body bolting upright while my hands keep him between my legs.

I collapse back into the soft cushions of the couch as he smiles at me, his beard glistening with my juices which gears up my insides for another round.

Kissing his way up to me, his beard itches my skin in the most delectable way, but when he gets to me, he's hesitant for a second, staring down at me.

I grab the back of his neck and pull him down to me, tasting myself on his mouth. A sweet thank you kiss turns ravenous and the tip of his dick is positioned at my center.

"Garrett," I say against his mouth. "Do you have anything?"

His forehead falls to my shoulder and he shakes it back and forth.

"No. You?"

If we were in my apartment, yes, but I don't pack condoms when I'm expecting a weekend alone.

"No."

"Shit." He sits up, his dick still hard and begging for me to wrap my pussy around it.

I'm throbbing with the expectation of how deep he'd fill me.

"How good of a maid do you have?" I ask.

He looks up, a smirk on his lips understanding my meaning.

Jumping up, he runs up the stairs and I follow, searching the other bedrooms.

I'm in the one furthest down the left side and he's in the master. The only sounds in the cabin are us opening and shutting every cabinet and drawer.

"Anything?" I yell out.

"No." The disappointment in his tone can't be missed.

"Me either."

We meet up in the middle bedroom until we're standing on either side of the bed naked, with matching frowns.

"I could run to the store," Garrett offers.

I glance at the alarm clock on the nightstand. "You'd have to go into Wet Rock."

And by the time he got there, they'd probably be closed.

"This might be the only time I wish we lived in a city," he grumbles.

I laugh, Garrett joking around isn't an everyday occurrence.

"Well." I crawl over the bed. "I did just have my exam last month and I haven't been with anyone." My finger runs up the patch of hair that runs from his navel to his joystick. At least I'm crossing my fingers that it brings me joy.

He looks down at me, contemplating his decision.

"I had a vasectomy."

I sit up on my knees and wrap my arms around his neck.

"Then I say we're good."

His two hands land on either side of my face. "I've never not used a condom."

I nod and he releases me. My lips travel to his ear. "Then I'd say you should fuck me right here."

He pushes me down on the bed and stares down at me. I

can't read his expression, and for a brief moment I think he's going to walk out the door without a goodbye, but he pulls my legs apart and slides me along the comforter to the edge of the bed.

"I want to start with me looking down at you."

His two hands play with my tits, his thumbs running over my nipples.

Reaching forward, I direct his dick to enter me and inch-by-inch he fills me. As soon as I'm fully wrapped around his hard length, a weird sensation hits me—peace and surrender almost.

He circles at first. A slow grind that ignites the bundle of nerves already on alert. The heat from his eyes scorch my skin and his calloused hands grip my hips. At first, he watches himself moving in and out of me until I arch my back and then his attention shifts back to my tits.

Never did I think Garrett's eyes would say so much as he watches me writhe under him. They're so filled with lust and raw need that I wonder if everything he said downstairs was true. Has he thought of me more than I realized?

"You're gorgeous." His hands leave my hips, molding my tits between his fingers. He manipulates them whichever way he wants. He doesn't know it, but nothing turns me on faster than when a man plays with my tits.

"God, Garrett," I pant, those nerve endings frenzied and ready for him to really fuck me.

He pulls out of me, flips me over, and moves me back to the edge of the bed.

Plunging back into me, his hands grab a hold of my tits like they're his anchors and he slides in and out of me, harder and faster with every thrust.

My arms struggle to hold my upper body up, even

though I'm fairly sure Garrett has me. My eyes drift shut and my head falls forward.

One hand leaves my breasts and he pulls me up until my back is pressed to his front while he continues to fuck me like he won't ever get enough. Turning my face to his, he kisses me and swallows down the cries of my orgasm as I pulse around his cock.

A second later, he stills inside of me, never slowing down our kiss. I desperately want to turn around and kiss him for the rest of the night.

I thought banging the big bad wolf would get him out of my system. I thought all the lust that fills me when he's near would disappear once I had him, but I never expected it to feel like *this*. I never expected to feel as though he was the missing puzzle piece all along and the two of us together somehow completed me.

Fuck.

I should leave.

I should forget this night, but instead, I ask, "How much longer until you're ready again?"

He chuckles into my back, his beard scratching my skin as he slowly withdraws from me.

"Usually I'd say twenty minutes, but with you, probably five."

He disappears into the bathroom and returns with a washcloth.

Yep, I need to leave. I definitely shouldn't be rolling over and allowing him to clean me up. There's no reason for me to be letting him lay over top of me on the bed so he can kiss me again.

"Make that a minute." He ends our kiss and I don't have to look down to know he's already becoming hard again because I can feel his length prodding my thigh.

Clearly my hand is a glutton for punishment because it doesn't listen to common sense as it ventures down to stroke him.

I'm a complete moron who deserves to get her heart broken because I already know that's exactly what Garrett Shaw will do to me.

The sun peeks into the master bedroom, waking me and I realize we never shut any of the shades last night. I sit up on the edge of the bed, my back to Charlie, and try to consider what the ramifications of my actions last night will be.

When I took her in my arms I was so mad that she thought she was anything but gorgeous. She's always been beautiful, even when she was eighteen, a newly graduated high school student that I should have never thought about as anything other than a little sister.

But when I was telling her all my forbidden fantasies, something took over and I had to kiss her. If only one time. Naively, I thought it would work her out of my psyche.

Pfft. She worked me like a sex slave last night and she's still infecting me like a virus that hasn't run its course. What started in the spare bedroom, moved to the kitchen while I fixed her an omelet. Who knew watching her slide the eggs off her fork would turn me on? Then we decided to take a dip in the hot tub since it was fixed and all. It wasn't in the plans to prop her on the edge and taste her once more but I couldn't resist. Turns out that white bikini is pretty much see through when it's wet. That blow job I denied earlier, happened at three in the morning while watching Fight Club after I asked Charlie what type of guy she liked—Brad Pitt or Edward Norton? Her response was to wrap her lips around my cock.

Good answer.

After she fell asleep on the couch and I carried her up to the master bedroom. Again, I told myself I shouldn't stay, but she pulled me in for a kiss and that was the end of that.

I stand up, needing to use the john, but as I round the edge of the bed to the bathroom, Charlie shifts and her left tit pops out from under the sheet.

It makes me sound like a complete cave man, but she has the best fucking rack.

Her eyes flick open and I pretend not to notice, high-tailing it into the bathroom, shutting and locking the door.

A second later, the doorknob jiggles and then the banging starts.

"I'm pissing here."

"Oh stop trying to use the whole asshole approach with me." Her voice is way too close and when I glance over my shoulder I know why.

The door is now open and she's standing there. Naked.

"Privacy!" I say and she laughs.

"The privacy train left when you tore off my bikini last night. Speaking of which, I think you should try boxer briefs." She's doing some sort of dance as she hops from one foot to the other.

While she's busy talking about my undergarments, my big fella can't get a drop of urine out. My morning hard-on coupled with Charlie's tits bouncing around is not conducive to certain bodily functions.

"Can we continue this conversation when I'm done?"

She smiles, her two hands holding her pussy as she continues to hop around the bathroom. "I'm about to push you out of the way."

"There are four other bathrooms in this place. Use one of those."

She sits on the edge of the whirlpool tub, crossing her legs and squirming. "What fun is that? Come on, hurry."

Knowing this is Charlie and obviously a lost cause, I turn away from the toilet and walk out of the room. The door shuts behind me.

Two minutes later it opens and Charlie is drying her hands on a towel.

"So, let me get this right, you get privacy but I don't?"

I leave the bedroom in search of my clothes downstairs.

"Well, I can't have you daydreaming about me peeing."

"But you can daydream about me peeing?"

She shrugs, her feet padding down the stairs behind me. "So, where's Syd?"

"She's at her grandparents." I pull up my jeans and search for my T-shirt only to look up and notice it on Charlie. I hold my hands out and she dodges my advance into the kitchen.

"Let me make you breakfast as a thank you for the multiple orgasms you bestowed upon me last night." She opens up the cabinet doors, finding a loaf of bread. My welcome package to the cabin always includes all the ingredients for a hearty breakfast. "Not sure why I thought these would be stocked. No one lives here."

I chuckle, watching her bottom lip droop.

"Maybe because of that omelet I made you last night."

She smiles. "That was a great omelet."

"Just the omelet?" I ask, my arms crossing over my chest.

"Who's looking for compliments now?" She slides up onto the counter, her legs parted enough for me to see she's still sans panties.

The small patch of hair teasing me.

"Shut your legs," I say, walking to the fridge.

I take out the bacon and then slide under her legs to grab the flatiron pan.

"Why? You don't like the view?" She cocks a brow, knowing damn well that it's a million dollar view.

She spreads her silky smooth legs further apart and like a Pavlov response, my cock is instantly straining the confines of my pants.

I take her knees in each of my hands and shut them. "Give me my T-shirt and go get dressed. I'll make us some BLT's since it's already eleven."

"I like this shirt. I think it fits me nicely."

I have to admit that some part of me enjoys seeing her wearing my shirt. As if it means she belongs to me or something. But we both know that isn't in the cards for us. Time to set things back to rights.

As I study her she rolls up the sleeves of my way-too-big-for-her T-shirt revealing a little more of her rockin' body.

"I can't lie, last night was nice. But it needs to be a one and done." I walk toward the fridge and she swings her legs out, locking me between them.

Now, if I really wanted to fight this, I have the strength to do so, but God her pussy is like a siren's call...once it has you, you're over and done with.

"So that's a no?" she asks, linking her ankles behind my back.

"We can't." My hands land on her legs.

"Fine. I don't beg a man to want me." She grabs the hem of my T-shirt and pulls it up over her head, revealing her perky tits and hard nipples. Then her ankles unhook from behind my back and she's jumping down, squeezing in between me and the counter before I can think a coherent thought.

Because I grab her wrist. Which if I was thinking, I wouldn't do.

And I swing her back my way, into my arms, allowing her breasts to crash against my bare chest.

"Fuck, I love feeling you pressed up against me."

She smiles. "I thought we weren't doing this anymore?" She's a good seductress because she arches her back just enough to show what I'm missing.

"We're asking for disaster," I say.

"I find it funny that you actually thought you could be one and done with me. Shame on you, Garrett Shaw."

I chuckle, my hands sliding down her back until the flesh of her ass is in my hands.

"That was the deal."

I haven't missed that she's yet to touch me. God, she's stubborn and hard-headed. She'll make me chase her for sure.

"Okay, then. One and done?" she asks.

I'll never admit to the stabbing sensation in my heart from her words. "Yeah."

She steps out of my arms, her ass falling out of my hand. "The master has spoken."

I stand in the kitchen watching her as she rounds the first step on the stairs, but the cabin door swings open and I might actually run out the back door. There's no possible way it's him.

"Shaw?" Vance's eyes narrow but his smile widens.

Charlie freezes on the first step and Vance, her brother, only has to take five more steps before he'll see his naked sister standing on the stairway.

"Vance? What are you doing here?" I ask.

He looks at the number on the cabin door. "Why are you here? I thought this was Charlie's cabin for the weekend?"

Vance's wavy dark hair is styled, he's wearing some sort of shorts that look like you'd have to take them to a dry cleaner and a button-down shirt with the cuffs rolled up. Man, Los Angeles might as well be a different country.

"The hot tub went out. I had to fix it," I say, feeling like a complete douche.

"And you do that shirtless?"

I eye Charlie again as she's tiptoeing up the steps.

Vance approaches and I take a deep breath for the wrath that's about to come down on us.

Charlie moves her burglar creep to an Olympic sprint and Vance rounds the corner right as she quietly shuts the door.

"Cut the shit, Shaw."

"How did you know she was here?"

Yes, I'm deflecting. Give me a break. Even though this guy in front of me looks like he'd pay me to not be a problem. The guy who used to solve problems with his fists has been replaced by a yuppie.

"What does it matter? Why are you in her kitchen with your shirt off?"

"Because he got it wet." Charlie comes out of the bedroom, fully dressed in yoga pants and a sweatshirt.

Vance turns toward his sister, a look of relief on his face.

"There you are." He laughs. Like bent over from the waist, holding his stomach, laughing. "For a minute I thought the Climax Cove gossip circle was hiding something."

"Please." Charlie walks down the stairs and hugs her brother while smirking over his shoulder. "You think if Garrett and I were hooking up anyone could keep that a secret?"

She eyes my T-shirt on the ground and I quickly snatch it from the floor, balling it up in my fist.

"I'll let the two of you catch up." I don't wait for an answer, but instead head out to the deck, pretending to grab my T-shirt from the railing, like it had been hanging to dry the whole time, I put it on.

The screen door opens and out walks Vance.

"Hey, friend." He puts out his hand in front of me. "Didn't mean to accuse you there."

Why, I just screwed your sister six ways to sideways last night and my dick is aching for her again?

I shake his hand and the first thing I realize is his callused hands are now smooth like Sydney's skin when she was a baby.

"I think you need to go climb some trees and axe some lumber. Man-up those hands."

He laughs.

"I'm an executive now. The most labor-intensive work I do is snap my fingers for a coffee." His eyes that look so much like his sister's milk chocolate ones, don't match the perma-smile plastered to his face. I can't help but think something is amiss, but who am I to say?

"What brings you back to Climax Cove?" I appraise his silver fancy watch, his clean-shaven face, his manicured nails. He hasn't returned in five years, why now?

"Thought it was time to visit the family." He shrugs.

"Someone sick?"

Charlie walks out of the cabin with three beers lodged between her fingers, showcasing her bartending skills.

After she hands them out, she places hers on the railing and pulls her sweater a little tighter.

Vance laughs. "No. Does someone need to be dying for me to visit?"

"Did Mom faint when she saw you?" Charlie intercedes and I choke down a laugh.

Vance's gaze shoots to me and his lips turn down, his cocky smile fading.

"No, she hugged me and told me I was her favorite child," Vance throws back. I forgot how well these two spar back and forth. They could compete in one of those stupid reality shows that are all over the fucking television these days.

"I'm fairly sure I'm the favorite." Charlie rolls her eyes and the two of them laugh.

"Nah, Garrett's probably still her favorite." Vance nods to me.

I forgot how much their mom loved me. Took care of me during those dark days and how did I repay her? I screwed her daughter.

"Well, I better get going. Sydney's waiting." I take the beer with me through the screen door.

"How is Sydney?" Vance follows behind me as I empty half my beer in the sink.

"She's twelve," Charlie informs him and Vance scoffs.

"Seriously? I have been gone a long time."

"Yeah, you have," Charlie says while eyeing me from behind her brother's back. "I still want to know why you picked now to come home?"

Vance runs his hand through his hair. "Just needed a break."

"Well, it's good to see you, buddy." I put my hand out. "We'll catch up soon."

Vance shakes my hand and then pulls me into a hug. "Sorry I thought you were nailing my sister. I saw red for a moment."

I nod, hating that I'm keeping a secret from him.

"I wouldn't blame you one bit." What the hell else can I say?

I walk out of the cabin a different man than I was when I showed up last night. A man who's gotten his first hit of a potent drug for free, but knows that anything more will cost him.

11

CHARLIE

Garrett leaves and my stomach sinks.

"Man, at first I thought you finally hooked Shaw." Vance laughs, sitting on the breakfast stool in the kitchen. I'll refrain from telling him about what a great lay Garrett was last night.

"I don't see why that's funny." I turn on the stove to cook the bacon that Garrett had intended to make for me.

"Please, that school girl crush you had? You used to drool over him." He sips his beer and I inwardly roll my eyes.

"Well, things have changed since you've been gone."

The bacon starts to sizzle in the pan and it's then that I realize what an appetite I worked up with Garrett last night.

My brother hasn't been home in five years and although we've all made trips down to see him in L.A., his schedule has long been too busy for us.

"Catch me up then." He rounds the counter and takes the tongs out of my hands.

Letting him have them, I prop myself up on the counter.

"Dane is with someone now."

His jaw drops. "Seriously?"

"Yeah, and she's great."

He nods. "Remember Marcus Kent?"

He hems and haws. "The one with the baby girl?"

"Yeah, he built a huge house up on the hill and he's on his way down the aisle too."

"Damn, how did all these single dads get chained to commitment?" He laughs because he'd never consider marriage.

I shake my head. "They went willingly."

He nods, placing the bacon on the paper towel covered plate.

"Do you want eggs?" he asks.

"No, I had my fill last night." I grin, but he doesn't ask me why.

We continue to talk about the town and although there isn't a ton that's changed, there's enough to show that he's no longer a native to Climax Cove but more of a transplant since he deserted us.

"Hey, I want to do some fun stuff while I'm here. The rapids, maybe hiking or mountain biking."

"How long will you be staying?" I chomp down on a piece of bacon.

"I don't really know yet. I'm on break, so I figured I'd stick around for awhile."

"And you're staying where?" I raise both eyebrows. My parents sold our childhood home last year and moved into a townhome with only two bedrooms—one for each of them since my dad is the king of all snorers.

"I don't know yet. You have an apartment, right?"

I nod. "But I have Marcus Kent, his girlfriend, and his daughter staying with me now."

"I'll ask Shaw. I'm sure he's willing to put up an old friend."

"No."

He draws back and looks over at me wondering what he's missing.

"Let me see when Marcus and Cat will be out. You know Garrett has Sydney and she's preteen and going through some stuff right now."

My reaction might've given something away, but I don't want my brother being at his house to solidify for Garrett that he's not supposed to be with me. My brother would win at a game he didn't even know he was playing.

"Okay, but cool if I stay here this weekend?"

My shoulders slump. "Fine, but the master's mine."

He laughs. "Great, I'll grab my bags from the rental car. Let's go to the rapids today. Call and see if they have any open reservations."

He walks out of the cabin and I tuck my legs into my body, contemplating my next move. Garrett hasn't admitted how much he needs me yet, so it's going to take a gentle nudge in the right direction. To hell with my brother.

***

HAPPY DAZE TAVERN IS OVERFLOWING WITH PEOPLE WHEN I arrive for my shift. After a weekend at the rapids and mountain biking, my entire body is sore. The one nice thing was that I didn't obsess about Garrett all weekend because I was too busy.

I glance to my left and there at a table in front of the windows are a bunch of the single dads, minus Garrett.

"Looking for your man?" Dane asks, filling two mugs of beer.

"What?"

"Don't pretend to be blonde now." He slides them to two of the dads waiting at the end of the bar and collects their money.

It really was a genius plan on his part to start this club and have his bar be the meeting place. What a way to boost a Monday night. Dane may come across as being a few sandwiches short of a picnic, but he's smarter than people give him credit for.

"That's offensive," Cat chimes in and I glance to my right to see her with Marcus.

"Are you allowing women into the group now?" I ask and Marcus laughs.

"Hell no." Dane drops an orange slice in Marcus's Blue Moon and then slides it over to him.

"I just dropped in before heading to the bakery." Cat smiles and looks over to Marcus with love overflowing from her eyes.

I may be slightly envious. Maybe.

"Speaking of which...didn't you have a request that Charlie doesn't bartend during the meetings?" Marcus eyes Dane who is now nodding his head.

"I completely forgot. You're off tonight," Dane says with a smile trying to sell me on the idea.

I narrow my eyes and place my hand on my hip. "I've been doing the meetings for years, why now?"

Chad enters from the backroom with his usual confused expression. "I thought only one of us was working tonight?"

My gaze moves over to the group of dads. "Which one was it?" I ask.

The door chimes and in walks Garrett. I watch him notice me and then shoot a look to Dane. Something passes between the two of them and then Dane is pleading with me to just leave it alone and head out.

"Garrett asked?" I whisper.

"What?" Cat whips her head to her side to look at Marcus.

"You know the rules babe, no information," Marcus responds, but Dane remains silent for a moment and that's when I know I'm right.

"Don't give me a hard time on this, okay?" Dane asks and I untie my apron and toss it on the top of the bar.

"I'm out," I say loud enough for the table of men to hear me and I square my eyes at Garrett, who doesn't make eye contact.

Spineless prick.

"Charlie!" Cat follows me out the door. "Hold up." She circles her arm through mine and detours me from heading to my Jeep and leads me across the street to the bakery.

Tears are lodged in the back of my eyes, desperately pleading to come out, but I'll never allow them to.

Once we're in the back of the bakery, watching Ava beat fondant to a nice shade of turquoise, Cat starts the conversation I knew was coming.

"What happened this weekend?" she asks, propped up on a stool on the other side of Ava.

I'm on the counter like usual, chomping on Ava's latest cookies—turkeys for Thanksgiving.

"What are you talking about?" I ask with a full mouth.

I have to admit, I never saw Garrett as a kiss and tell kind of guy.

"Garrett came over to Marcus' early Saturday morning and the two stayed on the deck for an hour."

"Why would that have anything to do with me?" I brush the cookie crumbs off my chest.

"Hey, you're mopping the floor," Ava points to me.

I slide off the counter and grab the broom from the back room.

"I may have opened a window in my studio and heard bits and pieces." Cat bites the inside of her cheek.

Damn it.

"What did you hear?"

"Yeah, what did you hear?" Ava beats the fondant with her rolling pin.

"That you guys slept together."

I throw my hands up in the air and the broom crashes to the floor. "What is this, high school?"

Cat stares at me with a puppy dog face. Ava's eyes widen and she continues to knead the fondant now looking between the two of us.

"Well, he was really nice with what he was saying. It's not like he was all like 'Charlie's easy and I love her rack.' It was more, 'what the fuck did I do and how do I move on from here' type of conversation."

I close my eyes briefly, picking up the broom again for something to do.

"We did sleep together. Five times."

"Shut Up!" Ava tosses the rolling pin to the side and sits on the stool. "You finally got him, huh?"

"That's the thing, I didn't. He told me the next morning it was never to happen again. That's why I'm confused."

Cat comes over to me, taking the broomstick out of my hands and guiding me to the stool she'd been occupying.

"He was really distraught," she says, cleaning up my mess.

Ava stands up and goes to the fridge. She throws a mound of cookie dough on the table.

"This calls for a pig out." She digs out three spoons, each of us taking one.

"Well, good. I'm glad he was distraught because I know he enjoyed it."

"It's sex, Charlie. Who doesn't enjoy sex?" Ava asks. Cat shoots Ava a look and she cringes. "No offense. I'm sure you're a sex kitten and all."

I shake my head. "It was more than sex, I know it." I lick some batter off my spoon.

"I get that I know nothing about his situation other than his wife passed away, but why hasn't he moved on? I mean it's been twelve years," Cat asks.

I shake my head. "I figure he's scared. But I know there was something there underneath it all. Feelings."

"I'm just playing devil's advocate here, but could you be reading something that isn't there?" Ava asks.

Maybe, I mean, I have liked him for most of my life. But no, with everything that's gone on in the past few weeks I know there's more to it.

"I truly don't think so," I say with the confidence I feel.

"I agree with Charlie. When he came over, he wouldn't look me in the eye when I answered the door," Cat says around a mouth full of cookie dough. "It wasn't *what* he said, it was his *tone*. I can't even describe it, but it was like he knew he made a mistake."

"A mistake by sleeping with her?" Ava asks, her spoon scooping another heap of cookie dough.

"No, he never said he wished he didn't do it. Never even questioned how it all transpired. He was only concerned about how he walked out on her."

That sliver of hope I've felt since he kissed me grows and I know what I need to do.

"That's it!" I slap the table.

"What's it?" Ava asks, her eyes tipping down in judgment.

"I just need to push him a little. At first I was going to wait for him to come to me, but nope, I'm going to pester him until he caves." I smile, happy with my revelation.

"You mean chase him?" Ava's judgmental tone comes out again.

"She technically already has him on the line, she's going to reel him in." Cat smiles, on board with my thinking.

Of course, us girls that go after what we want have to stick together.

"You're comparing it to fishing?" Ava asks.

"I'll drag him in inch by inch until he stops fighting me." I stand up and put my spoon in the sink, no longer able to eat with all the excitement swirling inside my belly.

"You go, girl!" Cat says placing her hand up in the air like I just made the winning spike in a volleyball game or something.

"I'm not sure about this, but tell me what you want me to do?" Ava asks like a good friend who doesn't agree with your plan, but will back you anyway.

"Right now I can handle it on my own I think, but I do need people to distract my brother." I bite my lip because although I was happy to have Marcus and Cat say they can move back into their house and Cat was more than happy to give her room to him, he's been stuck to me like glue since he returned.

"Done. I'll tell Dane that he should spend a lot of time with him while he's here," Ava offers.

I laugh because Dane and Vance used to be the two to get in the most trouble together.

"Be careful there," I warn her.

She giggles. "Toby and I have been trying to finish the

Harry Potter series, so having him preoccupied works in my favor."

"Thanks." I give both my friends a quick hug. "Okay, I need to go put my plan into action. I'll catch up with you two later."

I walk out of the bakery and my gaze flicks to the windows of Happy Daze Tavern to find someone staring out at me.

Garrett's eyes lock onto mine but then he looks away.

He has no idea what he's in for.

If he thought Charlie quietly pining away for him was hard to handle, wait until he meets Charlie who knows what she wants and goes after it.

I'm at the new build cabin on Foxfield when Charlie's lime green Jeep pulls up.

"Is that Charlotte Rose?" George asks, squinting his eyes.

I see now why he mismeasured the beams, the man needs his eyes examined.

"That's her Jeep."

Charlie walks up the plywood ramp with yoga pants and a sports bra on and a jacket over top that needs to be fucking zipped up. Her hair is pulled up in a high bun, the curls anything but tame.

"Hey, boys," she greets the workers and all saws and machinery halt as they watch her walk into what will be the kitchen once the special order granite comes in.

"What are you doing here?" I ask, grabbing a hold of her elbow and escorting her into the future game room.

"Oh, this looks nice." She ignores my hand and admires the room that's half finished.

"Charlie?"

"You should put a pool table here." She stretches her

arms out, giving me a full view of her double D's she's somehow managed to shove into that sports bra.

"I'm planning on it. Again, what are you doing here?"

She looks over at me with a sweet smile. "I brought you lunch. I was in Wet Rock for a conference this morning and thought I'd stop by on my way back."

This is what she wears to a conference? Somehow I think that first part was a lie. "Thank you." I take the cooler from her outstretched hands. "But you can't be here."

"Do I need a hardhat?" she asks, her eyes still perusing her surroundings.

"No. It's not that, it's just."

"Garrett," George calls into the room like he's afraid to see something he shouldn't. My dick might want to lift Charlie to the wall and pull down those yoga pants but I'm not a complete idiot. I'm not Dane.

"What's up, George?" I call out.

"The boys are going to take a lunch and give you some time."

I hadn't even noticed the machinery never turned back on. All I hear are footsteps out the front door and the sound of truck engines starting.

"Great, there goes three hours they should be working on the house." I shake my head.

"They didn't have to leave on account of me. I just thought you work so hard, you'd appreciate a good lunch."

"I think you're laying this sweet girlfriend thing on a little thick, don't you?"

She tilts her head to her shoulder, exposing the side of her neck. The impulse to lean forward and run my tongue from her collarbone to her earlobe burns inside me.

"Girlfriend?" she questions.

"You get what I mean."

"I don't think I do." She unhooks her hair from the ponytail band and shakes her hair out so the spirals lay across her shoulders.

Christ. I want it wrapped around my fist as my cock pushes into her mouth.

"Why are you really here, Charlie?" I sit down and open the cooler, finding two roast beef sandwiches, chips, and grapes.

"I already told you, to feed you."

I roll my eyes and she giggles, taking off her jacket.

"You're going to get cold if you take that off." I can't help but admire her taut stomach and smooth skin. And the way her waist curves in just above her hips.

"You could warm me up." She wraps her arms around herself, which only means her tits are smashed together and pressed higher up on her chest.

"Fuck, stop it."

She smiles and licks her lips. "What are you thinking about, Garrett?"

My eyes roam up and down her body and my dick twitches in my pants, pleading with me to let him come out and play.

"Nothing. Here." I hand her a sandwich. "Eat with me."

"I already ate, that's all for you so you can keep up your energy."

"Energy for?" I take a bite of the sandwich surprised to find she put horseradish in it.

How does she know so much about me?

"If you can't guess than we have a problem."

I exhale a loud sigh. "I told you it can't happen again. Especially with your brother back in town."

She waves me off. "Don't put yourself too high on that pedestal, I meant to finish this construction job."

"Oh."

She sits down on a paint bucket and crosses her legs.

"So, I'm here on another mission. The first boy and girl dance is coming up at the middle school."

"And?"

"I think Sydney would want to go, so, I'm here to offer my help."

"She won't be going." I bite into the second sandwich.

"Yes, she will."

I cock my head to stare at her for a moment until she realizes how serious I am. "No. She won't."

"She wants to go, Garrett." She stands up and places her hands on her hips. "I'll be over before five on Friday to take her dress shopping."

I let my shoulders droop and shake my head. "She's not going," I repeat.

Charlie pats me on the shoulder a serene smile on her face before she starts walking to the doorway.

"Where are you going?" I ask. "I thought we were having lunch."

"Huh." She stops and places her finger to her lips. "I don't remember you asking me to have lunch with you, but if you want a date all you have to do is ask."

Then she turns and walks out of the room. A second later her Jeep's ignition turns over and she drives away.

The woman is crazy. Seriously, certifiable.

CHARLIE

Friday can't come soon enough. Ava kept her word and when Dane isn't at the bar, he's with Vance. It's probably good for Dane though because neither Garrett or Marcus are adrenaline junkies like him. So, it's a win-win for everyone.

My finger presses the doorbell of the Shaw cabin.

I wait on the porch, looking over my shoulder to make sure that really was Garrett's truck I parked next to.

I ring it again and still no answer.

Hesitantly, I place my hand on the doorknob, surprised when it turns in my hand.

Bad idea I tell myself, but he should have just gotten home from work and Sydney should be ready to go.

"Hello!" I yell into the cabin and hear nothing in response.

It's silent and quiet, so I close the door.

"Hello!" I repeat but get the same answer I did moments ago—nothing.

I slowly walk around knowing I should just call or text

one of them instead of walking into their house but the worst I could find is Garrett naked and really, been there, hit that.

Hardly any pictures are hung on the wall except for some hunting photographs. A few of him and Sydney, but tucked away on one of the tables, is a wedding picture of him and Melissa.

She's sitting down on the grass and a clean-shaven Garrett is kneeling behind her. Both sport big grins, Melissa's two dimples prominent and on display. A stabbing sensation hits my gut.

What am I doing here?

Making a fool myself. That's what.

"Hey." Garrett's voice pulls me from thoughts of the happy couple. "Sorry, I was showering."

He walks down the stairway in jeans and barefooted. His long hair on top is pulled away from his face into a ponytail, the sides of his head shaved. Water glistens in his still damp beard.

"Taking your chances with the door open," I say.

"I only have to worry if black bears somehow recently developed opposable thumbs." He stops at the edge of the couch and the scent of his cologne lingers between us.

My eyes shoot to the wedding picture and that self-doubt that rarely ever seeps into my pores drowns me.

"Hey now, Krystal and her gang might surprise you." I laugh and he smiles.

Krystal is the single mom in Climax Cove who always seems a little desperate to find someone. She had her eye on Marcus. That is until Cat came along.

"I'm not Marcus." He walks forward. "Want a drink?"

I secure my purse on my shoulder. "Where's Sydney?"

He huffs. "She should be home in about fifteen. She just texted me."

"Okay." I stand in the doorway between the kitchen and the family room. It's clean, no dirty dishes. Sydney's report card is on the fridge, bananas on the counter. No knick-knacks of roosters or decorations to make the space homey.

He opens the stainless steel fridge, grabs two beers and nods toward the balcony.

"Come out back. The sun is about to set."

I follow, wondering why he's being so nice to me.

We walk through the sliding doors and there's no table, but outdoor furniture with orange cushions on them. He sits in the chair and I take the couch, staring up at the sky painted in burnt oranges and vibrant yellows.

"It's getting colder," I remark, suddenly losing all enthusiasm after seeing the picture.

"Yeah." He sips his beer. "I have to finish up the cabins before Christmas."

"Do you ever take time off?"

He hems and haws for a second. "Kind of. I usually try to solidify the deals and nail down the drawings during January and February. It's not vacation time, but work is light."

"Must be nice."

"What are you complaining about? You have summers off."

I nod. "Yeah and then I took a job at the camp."

He's silent for a second. "I'm sorry that Vance ruined your weekend at the cabin."

I look over, sipping my own beer, putting my feet up on the ottoman.

Garrett never looks my way, instead he focuses his eyes to the sky.

"Oh, it's nice to have him back."

Garrett sits up, placing his elbows on his knees. "He should be here shortly. We're going out to some club in Wet Rock tonight."

I nod like an idiot. I shouldn't care, but I want to know why he's willing to go trolling for pussy, but I'm not good enough for a repeat performance.

"Sounds like fun," I somehow manage to say even though my teeth are grinding together.

"With your brother, I'm sure it will be."

I stand up with the beer in my hands. "I think I'm going to text Sydney and I'll just pick her up wherever she's at." My hand is on the door handle of the screen door when his chest presses to my back.

"Charlie."

"What?" I focus forward, but I feel his chest move, his hot breath tickling my neck. "I should have never crossed over the line with you. I'm sorry."

I whip around and narrow my eyes. "You're sorry?"

He nods. "I am. I just ..."

"Why?"

"Why what?" he asks, backing up now since my finger is poking him in the chest.

"Why not me? Am I not good enough for you? Well, let me tell you, you aren't some prize package on my doorstep delivered by Ed McMahon and Publisher's Clearing House, okay? I'm a good catch."

"The best."

"I'm educated, I'm funny, I'm attractive, I have great tits and most of all I'm willing to take on all your fucking baggage."

He stops at the balcony and holds up his hands.

"No argument."

I nod. "Good." I turn on my heels until I realize he agreed with me. "Wait, what?"

"I agree with you. Any guy would be lucky to have you. Hell, I'd be lucky to have you, but circumstances aren't in our favor. I have responsibilities, you have a whole future ahead of you. One you should experience without a guy who can't offer a commitment."

I nod slowly. My head moves up and down as the anger fills my veins like venom. "That's right. No commitment. No getting hurt again, right? Just go through life numb and hope you never have to *feel* anything ever again. I'm sorry you lost the one woman you truly loved and maybe I'm an idiot for trying to weasel my way into your heart, but you're fooling yourself by believing that you don't want a commitment. You're just scared. You're letting fear run your life."

I open the screen door and slam it behind me, only to find Sydney standing in the kitchen staring at me.

"Come on. Let's go get a dress." I walk past her and open up the front door, finding my brother on the doorstep.

"How come I keep finding you with Shaw?" His fingers thread through his hair and he shakes his head.

I glance behind me, not finding Sydney. "Because I was a fool who thought I could crack his impenetrable shell."

By the time I start up my truck, Sydney's climbing in. I don't wait for Vance or Garrett to stop us but peel out of his driveway.

"I'm sorry about my dad," Sydney whispers once we're on our way to Wet Rock.

"Why?" I shoot her a fake smile. One that suggests my heart isn't breaking in half and leaking all the hope and excitement I had for the future out of it as we speak.

"You like him." She takes a deep breath. "He's just never

going to get over her." I watch her swipe her finger under her eyelid.

"Hey, how about we get that dress and then the two of us go to dinner?"

"I'd love that." Sydney smiles even with tears filling her eyes.

"Explain to me why I keep finding my sister here," Vance says as he walks into my kitchen.

I'm just coming in from the deck and I look at him then throw my bottle into the recycling bin.

"Because I slept with her."

It seems to take Vance a minute before the words I speak unscramble and make sense in his brain.

I hold my arms out to my sides. "Take your best shot. I deserve it."

Vance shakes his head, his chest heaving, face red. "The cabin?"

"Yeah."

"And?"

"And what?"

"Are you a couple?"

"No. It'll never happen again."

His fist cocks back and he nails me right in the eye. "Fucking asshole!"

My foot slams on the floor as my hands cover my eyes. "Motherfucker."

"Don't be a goddamn baby. You deserved it."

I know I deserved it, but that doesn't mean it doesn't hurt like a bitch.

"To all hell." My head falls back between my shoulder blades.

"How could you sleep with her if there was no possibility of a relationship?" Vance opens the fridge and grabs a beer for himself, sitting down at the table.

"So you wouldn't have hit me if I'd proposed?" I grab my own beer and sit down at the table, still blinking to get rid of the water pooling in my eye.

"I still would've taken the opportunity to hit you, I just wouldn't be as pissed at you." He shakes his head back and forth. "You know she's always liked you."

I nod. "I know."

"Do you? Because I saw her face when she opened that door. You've hurt her."

One vein in his neck is pulsating and if I say much more he's going to nail me again.

"I thought we'd get each other out of our systems."

"What are you nineteen? That never works."

I stare down at the kitchen table. The kitchen table I made myself. I spent hours carving and staining this thing after Sydney went to bed. Filling my time so I wouldn't feel how lonely I'd become.

Vance leans back in his chair. "You know she's never coming back, right?"

"Charlie? Yeah."

"No. Charlie is a lovesick puppy dog when it comes to you. She sees something others don't."

I nod. "Thanks for the compliment."

"I meant Melissa. She's dead bro. She's not coming back."

I stand up so fast my chair tips over. "You think I don't know that? I get that I'm alone. I've gotten that the last twelve years, but I'm not about to put myself in the position to feel that kind of pain again."

"You've hooked up with women before. Every time you've come down to L.A. in fact, and you didn't have a problem then." Vance raises his eyebrows in question. "Why didn't you just go to Portland or somewhere else and screw some stranger until you were satisfied? Why did you have to go fuck around with my sister?"

His question is valid.

"I don't know."

"Yes, you do."

I turn and grab the first thing I find in the freezer then sit back down with a bag of frozen corn on my eye.

"No, I don't."

Vance reaches over and smacks my forehead with his palm. My head flies back.

"Think with that big noggin," he says.

"What are we even talking about?" Damn, I underestimated his scrawny new L.A. body. He's still got some power behind that fist.

"We're talking about the fact you like her, too. I tried to turn a blind eye, believe me, but you do. The way your eyes always search her out. The way you'd come down to L.A. and ask me a million questions about her when you live in the same damn town. The way you purposely go to Happy Daze when she works." He shrugs his shoulders in a way that dares me to argue any of his points.

"Let me guess, you've been talking to Dane?"

Fucking Dane and his big mouth. What is said in the Single Dads Club meeting is confidential.

"I did, but only because the whole scene in the cabin didn't sit right with me. I asked him what I was missing. He only said that Charlie is still pining away and you're still acting like you don't notice."

I scratch my head, buying time. "Even if I like her, it's inevitable what would happen. I'm not built to truly love someone anymore, which would leave Charlie in a worse position than if I stop it now."

He stands up and shakes his head.

"Fine. I'm not going to fall to my knees and beg you to date my sister. Someone else will come along and you'll miss out. In the meantime, let's go find you some bar slut to hook up with." He tucks in his chair and walks to the front door.

Fucking Roses. I feel like I've been sucker punched for the third time in fifteen minutes.

A WHILE LATER, I'M SITTING AT SOME RESTAURANT IN WET Rock with Dane and Vance. Lucky Marcus got out of it saying that Lily was sick.

I hold my hand out in the air. "Let me just say before the night begins...I'm not talking about Charlie, commitment or anything else."

"Who wants to talk about Charlie?" Dane looks at Vance. "I see her and her smart mouth enough."

Vance nods. "Why would I want to talk about my sister while I pick up chicks?"

"Hey," Dane raises his hands in the air. "No chicks for this guy."

Vance hits him in the stomach. "I can't believe you've actually settled down."

Dane holds up his left hand. "No ring yet."

"Yet is the key word," I say and look at Vance. "Have you met Ava?"

He nods. "And I've eaten her cookies." Vance winks.

"Stay away from her MUFF-ins, got it?" Dane's lips get tight and he narrows his eyes at Vance.

Vance holds his hands up in the air in mock defense, laughing. "I agree," he says. "Might as well put a ring on it. Regardless, she seems cool and man, can she bake."

Dane's smug look on his face says it all. The man has spun a one eighty.

"Just remember to stay away from her MUFF-in." He slaps Vance on the back.

"Yeah, yeah, I got it. She's cute and all but I don't take other guy's girls so relax."

"She's not cute, she's fucking smokin' hot," Dane argues and I sip my beer, ignoring their carrying on.

"Hey." Vance leans forward. "You've been spotted."

I follow his gaze and glance over my shoulder, finding a redhead and brunette checking us out. They give us a small wave.

"I'll do you a solid and be your wingman tonight," he says.

The times I've visited Vance have usually been filled with partying which meant girls, drinking and usually surfing or motor crossing. Those times happen spontaneously and weren't planned like they're trying to do now. They either think I won't fuck one of the girls behind me because I'm so obsessed with Charlie, or they think I will and it'll be a good night for both Vance and myself. I may not be able to be with Charlie, but you don't trade down a week after the best fuck of your life.

But I'd love nothing more than to call their bluff.

"Fine, but I'll take the redhead. Reminds me less of your sister." I don't wait for his reply, but stand up, grabbing my beer.

"You're taking the brunette." Vance comes alongside me, swinging his arm over my shoulders.

We're two steps away from the girls when Vance's phone rings in his pocket. He doesn't bother to answer it, which seems odd. Every other time I've visited him in L.A. he's had that thing attached to his ear.

"You gonna answer that?"

"No. We have ladies waiting."

Then my phone vibrates in my pocket and unlike Vance, I stop and pull it out.

Sydney.

"What's up, Syd?" I answer and the faces of the two girls in front of us distort and they walk away.

Vance throws his hands up in the air with a 'what the fuck' look.

"Dad. Charlie had an allergic reaction." I hear car engines and people in the background.

"Where are you?" I signal to Dane who throws down cash on the table and catches up to us as I reach the doors, Vance trailing behind.

"We're at the hospital."

"In Wet Rock?" I ask.

"Yeah."

I hear Charlie in the background saying she's fine.

"She's breathing okay again, but they want to watch her for a few hours." When did my girl start sounding so grown up?

"I'm fine!" Charlie screams. "Can I talk to your dad?"

Dane starts up his Jeep and I cover the phone. "Wet Rock Memorial," I whisper and Dane nods.

"Hey," Charlie says when she gets on the line. "I don't even know what it was. Thank goodness for Sydney's epi pen."

I make a mental note to replace Sydney's just in case she gets stung by a bee.

"We're on our way," I say.

"Okay, you can grab Sydney. We did manage to get the dress before all hell broke loose though." I hear the smile in her voice. "It's very pretty and don't worry." She lowers her voice. "Not too much skin shows."

I chuckle and Dane cocks his head in my direction so fast I point to the front where he should be looking.

"Hold tight. Almost there."

"Take your time, we're watching Gilmore Girls while we wait. Jesse just arrived back in town."

"Yeah, I don't understand anything of what you just said."

We hang up and Vance turns around. "She okay?"

"Is she allergic to anything?" I ask because it seems crazy that at twenty-six she would have a reaction so severe.

"Charlie? No. I thought it was Sydney." Vance's face scrunches up. "Should I call my mom?"

"Nah. I talked to her, she's fine, but they're holding her for a few hours."

He purses his lips for a second. "Then I'll hold off on calling in the brigade."

"Call her, I'd love some meatballs." Dane elbows him and we all laugh.

Mrs. Rose came to Climax Cove as a foreign exchange student. She married Mr. Rose and became a native, but her Italian roots run deep. Meaning the Roses were the place to go for food when we were starving teenagers.

"Come over. She's been cooking up a storm since I've been back."

"You don't have to ask me twice." Dane turns into Wet Rock Memorial, and I can't stop the memories from flooding my mind.

MELISSA HAD BEEN OVERDUE WITH SYDNEY AND THE DOCTOR HAD suggested we have sex to bring labor on. Not that I minded after months of her saying she was too tired or felt too fat.

I quickly realized why the doctors get paid the big bucks because not even eight hours later, I was driving into the parking lot of the hospital with a screaming Melissa clinging to the door handle.

"Slow down, G!" she yelled as I practically took the corner on two wheels.

I stopped at the Emergency entrance, hastily threw the truck in park and went to help her out.

"I got it." She shooed me away and wobbled through the sliding doors.

A nurse came with the wheelchair before the doors shut behind her and told me to park the truck, that she wasn't going to have the baby right then.

I did as I was told because that was the person I was. I nodded like the agreeable boy my mom raised and parked the truck.

When I returned to the hospital it didn't take long to locate Melissa—I just followed her screams.

I rushed into the room, and stood at her side and held her hand, even with my circulation being cut off numerous times.

"The baby is coming faster than expected," the young doctor said. "Are you ready, Melissa? It's almost time to push."

The machine kept beeping but I never questioned it. Melissa kept whimpering but I figured that was normal for a woman in labor.

Doogie rolled his chair between her legs and a nurse came to the other side of Melissa.

She smiled over to me. Her kind eyes were trusting. Pulling Melissa's leg back, she instructed me to do the same.

"Okay, Melissa, push," Doogie said.

And Melissa did. She looked over at me, periodically squeezing her eyes shut.

"Hold up, Melissa, don't push for a second." Doogie's palm was up in the air as his head was buried between my wife's legs.

"I need to push," Melissa pleaded with him, but his hand remained up.

"Doctor, is everything okay?" That sweet nurse asked in a light voice so no one would be alarmed.

"Amy," he called over his shoulder to another nurse in the room there to assist him.

She looked down and then leaned close. Melissa's panicked gaze locked on mine and I squeezed her hand reassuringly.

"What's going on?" I asked, but silence filled the room.

"Get the OR ready and page Dr. Stein."

I was so concerned with the doctor and nurse exchange, I never noticed that Melissa's hand slipped from mine. Mindlessly, my attention still on the medical staff, I searched for it, finding it limp.

The machine kept beeping.

"We're going now," Doogie yelled and the other nurse tried to give me that sweet smile, but the flash of fear in her eyes brought me back to the moment and the reality of what was happening.

Melissa wasn't screaming, or pleading to push. I would've done anything for her to swear, to yell, to call me every name in the book, but she just lay there.

"Mr. Shaw, I need you to stay here." The nurses got the bed rolling and they rolled her out.

I stepped forward to follow, but Doogie stopped me. "Your wife's blood pressure is dropping, the baby is in distress. We need to do an emergency C-section. Stay here and someone will be back."

He ran out of the room and I ran after him until he went through a door I had no access to.

I had made no calls because Melissa was dead set about it being just us when she had the baby. She wanted to enjoy that special moment with the three of us before the chaos of our families and friends joined in.

I sat in that plastic chair outside the operating area until Doogie returned with the news that changed my life, and the life of my newborn daughter, forever.

"GARRETT," VANCE KNOCKS ON THE WINDOW AND I LOOK UP to see him staring at me through the glass, brows drawn.

Dane's a few steps back, understanding written on his face. He pulls Vance away from the door and the two exchange a few words.

I open the door, pushing the memory back.

"Why don't I just go grab Syd and bring her out?" Dane offers as he follows me through those same Emergency Room doors as twelve years before.

"No. I want to check on Charlie, too." I don't wait for either one of them, but they jog to catch up with me.

"I'll handle Charlie. Really, let Dane and I go in. You stay." Vance places his hand on my chest to stop me.

"Do you think I'm going to lose it or something?" I ask them and they both shake their heads.

"I just don't want you to have to go through it."

"I'm fine, okay. Let's just get this over with."

I swallow down the agony of being here again and ignore the haunted memories trying to fester inside me. I face the memory of the worst day of my life head on, but right before I reached Charlie's room, I overhear them talking and that's when my heart plummets so far down into my stomach, I'd be surprised if it's still beating.

Sydney and I have been at the hospital for an hour now, watching Gilmore Girls on the television. She's been quiet, sitting on the chair beside me. Her dress for the dance hanging up on the back of the door.

"You and Dad are kind of like Lorelai and Luke." She shyly looks over at me, judging my reaction.

I raise my eyebrows. "Why would you say that?"

She tucks her legs under her body. "Because you both like each other, but refuse to admit it."

"I'm not so sure about that."

Here I thought Sydney was too wrapped up in her own life to notice.

She shrugs. "You both watch each other when you think the other isn't looking."

I bite down my smile, but her admission does make my heart pitter patter a little.

"Your dad isn't ready."

"To move on?" Sydney asks.

I nod. This is probably not an appropriate conversation

to have with her, but she's way more observant than I think Garrett realizes.

"From my mom you mean."

"Yeah."

"I never even knew her."

I nod. Everyone in Climax Cove knew about the tragedy of Melissa's death.

She picks at the lint on her jeans. "It's weird to be half of someone you've never met."

I nod.

"Did you know her?" she asks me.

"Yes."

"Did you like her?"

When she and Garrett would come over to my parents' house, she seemed quiet and reserved, except with Garrett, but who am I to really say? I was young. And I had a crush on Garrett so in my eyes no one was worth his attention.

"Yes. Although, I didn't know her well."

She sits for a minute or so, her eyes moving from the television and then to me.

"I'm worried about him."

I shift to face her. "How so?"

"That I'll go off to college and then he'll realize he's let his life pass him by."

I laugh. "Has anyone ever told you that you're very wise for your years?"

"My nana says it. She blames it on my dad because he never hid anything from me." She smiles as though she's proud that her dad never did.

"I think your dad is living." I sit up in the bed and grab the water the nurse brought in for me. "He's started a great company, has friends, activities he likes doing on his off hours."

She shrugs in that typical preteen, whatever way. "He has no one special. I hear him at night, either in our garage building his ... things, or he's watching television in the dark all by himself. He seems lonely sometimes."

Tears form in my eyes because I love the way Sydney loves her dad so much that she's noticed things like that. Things that a lot of twelve-year-olds would disregard because they're too busy thinking about their own issues.

"All in due time I'm sure."

"Charlie...Miss Rose."

"Call me Charlie outside of school."

She smiles. "It's been twelve years. How much longer does he need?"

"No one knows that but him. But he will move on eventually. I'm sure of it."

Another few minutes go by and the show goes to commercial.

"Will you promise not to give up?" she says it so fast, I almost miss it.

"Not give up?" I ask.

"On him. Don't give up on him."

I smile and sip my water to distract myself from truly thinking about how long I've already waited for him.

"Oh, Sydney, you'll come to realize, what is meant to be will be. There's no rushing your dad and maybe when the time is right we'll get together, but if it's not me, I'm almost positive he'll find the right person."

As gut wrenching as that was to admit, it's the truth. I could be fooling myself with what I feel for Garrett and what I think he could feel for me—if he allowed himself. But the possibility exists that he may never recover from Melissa's death.

"I hope you're right."

"Hey, I'm older than you. That means I should know more." I laugh and she joins me until a big body stands in the doorway, stealing our attention.

"What the hell did you do?" Dane's voice booms into the room. His eyes set on me as he walks in. "Way to save her life," he says to Sydney and holds up his hand for a high five. "You should ask for an iPad or something big."

Sydney giggles. "Hey, Uncle Dane."

Dane plops down on my bed, making my own body bounce around.

"Way to take care of the patient," I deadpan and he pats my leg.

"Tell me." He leans in. "Did you plan all this to get his attention?"

I give him a bored look. "Yes, jackass, I decided to magically make myself allergic to something and then when my throat closed up and I couldn't breathe, I thought yeah, this will make him realize I'm the one." I smack him over the head.

Holding his head with his palm he says, "Jeez, I was just asking. You put a crimp in boy's night."

"So, sorry. Anything I should talk to Ava about?" I ask like the smart ass I am.

"The fact he sat there and told us how great monogamy is? No." Vance walks through the door, eyeing Sydney. Walking toward her, he waves his hand in response. "Hey, I'm your Uncle Vance."

"Yeah, you lost your uncle status when you hightailed it to Los Angeles and thought you were better than us," Dane hollers and then smacks my leg like I'm in on the joke.

Vance glances over his shoulder and I wonder how many times a day Dane gets that annoyed stare from my brother.

"I remember. Hi." Sydney waves her hand.

She straightens herself in the chair, her feet falling to the ground.

"Oh, Syd, is this the dress?" Dane hops off the bed and starts pulling up the plastic surrounding the garment.

Sydney stands and meets Dane there. She waits for him to reveal it and then bites her lip waiting for Dane's response.

Dane being Dane takes the hanger down, holding the dress up to his body and sauntering around the room. "I'm Sydney Shaw," he says in a high-pitched voice. "Don't touch me otherwise my bear of a dad will pummel you!"

"Seriously, doesn't Ava want you home?" I ask.

Sydney smacks him in the shoulder and takes the dress from his hands.

"Jesus, Dane." Garrett enters the room with his hands stuffed in his pockets. His face is on the pale side and all his body language is stiff.

His gaze searches the room and finds me, and I swear he relaxes just a smidge.

"There's the big bear now." Dane smiles over at me. "And for your information, Ava and Toby are bonding over Harry Potter right now."

"You don't want to watch the movies?"

"They're reading. I'm not sure I'm built to sit in a room and listen to someone *else* do all the talking."

Everyone in the room laughs. Vance sits down in the chair next to me and says, "That's the truth."

Garrett approaches Sydney, wrapping his arm around her shoulders. "I'm proud of you." He kisses her temple and she beams up at him. "The dress is very pretty."

"Thanks, Dad."

When Garrett looks back up, the three of us try to act like we weren't watching them.

"Where's your Jeep?" he asks me. No hello, or how are you doing. Nope, straight to business.

"It's at the mall, outside Macy's."

"Where are your keys?" he asks and I know he's going to leave me here because he doesn't want to be here. I'm not naive enough to think it didn't take him a lot of courage to walk through the hospital doors.

"In my purse."

Dane, Vance, and Syd's heads volley between Garrett and me during our conversation.

Without another word, he walks to my purse and digs out my keys.

I steel myself for him to leave with the excuse of going to get my car. My heart is already hardening with the thought.

"If you can bring it back here, they should release me in a few hours and I can drive myself home."

"I'll drive you, sis," Vance says, propping his feet up on the bed and grabbing the remote like he's making himself comfortable.

Garrett throws my keys into Vance's lap.

His gaze flickers away from the television to Garrett.

"You and Dane go pick up the Jeep, drive it back here and then you can pick up Sydney and drive her home."

"How about a please and a thank you? I hope you have better manners than your dad, Syd." Dane shakes his head and slides off the bed. He leans over me, kissing me on the cheek. "Next time fake a coma or something. Bigger is better. Just ask Ava."

I hit him in the chest and he winks at me and chuckles on his way toward the door.

"You okay with this?" Vance whispers from beside me. "I can stay." I smile at my brother's over protectiveness.

"Let's go, Vance. Stop the big brother act. Charlie could probably kick your ass. She's a big girl now." Dane winks at me again.

Vance gives him a fleeting look before focusing his attention back on me.

"I'm good," I say.

His chest rises and falls with a deep breath.

"I figured. Okay, I'll be right back." He squeezes my shoulder and then stands, the two of them walking out the door.

"Remember Days of Thunder?" Dane's loud voice bounces back to us from the hallway. "Let's grab some wheelchairs and I'll race you to the exit."

"Yeah, I'm not in the mood to be arrested tonight," Vance says and then their voices fade away.

Garrett takes Vance's seat next to me and looks up at the television.

"What is this?"

"Gilmore Girls," Sydney and I say unison.

He shakes his head but never tries to use the remote to change the channel.

The nurse comes in after a few minutes, checking the vitals they have me hooked to.

"I apologize for the wait. The doctor will be here soon."

"I really think I'm fine."

She pats my forearm in a grandmotherly way, although she's more likely my mother's age.

"We can't be too careful. It would be nice if you wrote down what you ate right before your episode."

"I told you I was at a Chinese restaurant in the mall."

She cringes. "You might want to eventually call over there and find out what ingredients are in the dish you ate."

"I'll call," Garrett's deep voice rumbles through my body.

"Hello," Nurse Kate says to Garrett. "What a beautiful family." She stares from Sydney to Garrett, lastly smiling at me.

"Oh. We're n—"

"Like I said, the doctor will be in soon." She doesn't wait for an answer from me, but leaves the room, leaving the door open only a small crack to give us some privacy.

"I'll tell her later," I say to Garrett, but he shrugs.

"Sydney." Garrett stands. "Take a walk with me."

She throws him a grumpy look, obviously invested in the Gilmore Girls and I laugh. Reluctantly, she stands.

"We'll be right back." He places his hand on her back and leads her out of the room.

I'm thinking I should've taken Vance up on his offer. At least he would have remained in the room.

Over the next fifteen minutes, I check my phone about twenty times. I try to get into Gilmore Girls, but it's not holding my interest because I want to know where Garrett and Sydney went. None of my friends are posting anything interesting on Facebook, Instagram or Snapchat. I'm about to open my Kindle app on my phone and read a book when the two of them return.

Sydney has her hands full of junk food and Garrett holds a pack of playing cards.

"You remember how to play Gin Rummy?" he asks, sliding the chair Sydney was sitting in closer to the bed.

He positions the table across my bed lower and for the next hour, the three of us play Gin Rummy, while Sydney gobbles down enough junk food that it could potentially land *her* in the hospital.

16

Talk about sucking it up for the sake of fatherhood. Watching your baby girl get all primped and primed so she can be mauled by young boys who are going through puberty and probably beat off to Victoria's Secret magazines. To make matters worse, Charlie is here curling Sydney's hair. The two of them are giggling up in the bathroom with the door closed.

Another problem is that Charlie showed up here with leggings, a short skirt and a tight V-neck shirt that makes it impossible not to remember what it felt like to have her tits in my hands.

The night of her allergic reaction, Charlie slept in our downstairs guest bedroom that Nana and Papa use when they babysit Sydney and I'm out of town. Knowing that only fifty footsteps separated us all night made it impossible to sleep.

Hearing Sydney's confession about fearing I'd die alone was a real eye opener. Not that she said that in so many words, but I got the gist. The last thing I want is for my daughter to not live her life to the fullest because she's scared of me being alone. I want her out there conquering her fears. I don't want to be the anchor that's constantly dragging her down.

Is that why I agreed to stay with Charlie in the hospital? I'm not sure.

Is that why I took Syd to the vending machines and bought food and found a pack of cards from the nurse's station to play with? I'm not sure.

The only thing I know for sure is that I'm not sure what I'm doing. How's that for ironic? I know I like being with Charlie. I know I don't want to shy away from her anymore. But the problem is I also know that I need to figure out exactly what I do want before actively pursuing her because there's no coming back from me hurting her. And the thought of hurting her is like a jagged knife ripping through my stomach.

"Are you ready?" Charlie's sweet voice says from over the banister.

My gaze shifts from the television up to her and I kind of wish she wasn't wearing leggings.

"I suppose." I stand and round the back of the couch.

Sydney's friends should be here soon and then she's spending the night at Chloe's house.

Charlie disappears for a second and then Sydney walks out of the bathroom and down the stairs.

The black dress is short but not too far above the knee. Her arms are covered. Neckline up to her collarbone.

All in all, I approve.

Her hair is down and in curls, with the front pinned back.

I'm game for this until I see her face.

"Whoa, what's that?" I point to her eyes.

"Just a little eye shadow and mascara." Charlie tosses off my concern.

"I said no makeup."

Sydney's shoulders sag and her gaze shoots to Charlie.

"Well, she's twelve and it's a dance." She digs through her purse and then hands Syd a bottle of something glossy.

"I'm the father remember?"

Charlie nods. "That's hard to forget."

"Dad, it's just a little. I'm not wearing red lipstick or foundation or anything."

"For the record, you'll never wear red lipstick," I say to Syd before directing my attention to Charlie. "I thought we agreed?"

Charlie smirks. "No. You said no makeup, but either I do it here or she does it in the middle school bathroom."

I look to Sydney waiting for her to refute what Charlie is accusing, but she remains silent and breaks eye contact with me.

"I don't like the idea of you two working together." I weave between them as they laugh at me.

The doorbell rings as I'm grabbing a beer for myself, so I set it on the table and head to say goodbye to my girl who looks way closer to sixteen than I'd care to admit.

Chloe and Sasha are in the doorway, each wearing dresses that can't have much more material to them than a scarf does and a shade of lipstick you'd see on someone ten years their senior.

Charlie shoots me a smug look.

I suppose I should be grateful—it could be worse. I take the deep breath I need to get through this.

"Okay, bye." Syd waves her hand, but I approach her.

"Hi, Chloe and Sasha," I say.

"Hi, Mr. Shaw. Miss Rose." They greet both of us.

"Have fun girls." Charlie's hip leans on my entry table that has her purse on it.

"Text me when you get back to Chloe's, okay?" I say to Sydney. Pulling out my wallet, I hand her a twenty.

"Thanks, Dad." She rises on her tiptoes and kisses my cheek and I hug her into my body, wishing she could stay my little girl for a while longer.

She leaves my arms and then walks over to Charlie for a hug.

"Thank you for your help," she whispers.

"You're welcome," Charlie says, her eyes finding mine over Syd's shoulder.

Chloe and Sasha stand in the doorway, eyeing our exchange.

"Go, have fun." Charlie nudges her closer to the door.

One last goodbye and I wave at Chloe's dad as the girls walk toward his truck.

"Why is Miss Rose at your house?" I hear Sasha ask, glancing over her shoulder at the doorway.

"She's friends with my dad."

"Like friends or like close friends?" Chloe asks and all three of the girls look over right before they get to the truck.

Sydney shrugs. "I don't even think they know."

Once the taillights are heading down my driveway, I shut my door, but Charlie has her coat on and her purse slung over her shoulder.

"Are you leaving?" I ask.

"Yep." She slides by me, the smell of her perfume causing my dick to twitch.

"I thought maybe we could have dinner or go out?"

She lets a sarcastic laugh loose, her back to the door. "Why?"

"Why does there have to be a reason?" I ask her, not ready to put everything out on the table.

"Are you asking me on a date?" she asks, jutting out her hip.

"Why do we have to classify it?" I run my hand down my beard.

Why do women have to make everything so damn difficult?

"Because Garrett, if you want to have dinner with me, then I'm guessing you want my company and that sir, is called a date."

I shake my head. "Fine, Charlie Rose, will you have dinner with me?"

"No." She turns the doorknob in her hand and opens the door.

"No?"

"No." She walks up to me, her chest pressing into mine. "You're a big boy, Garrett and it's time that if you want something, you go after it."

She shuts the door behind her and I hear her Jeep rev up, driving away a minute later.

What the fuck just happened?

17

CHARLIE

I slam my front door, to find Ava sitting on the couch.

"What are you doing here?" I ask, annoyance in my tone.

"Oh, I'm sorry. I thought I still wrote part of that rent check every month." Ava stands up, grabbing a bowl from the table and moves to the kitchen.

"Sorry. It's just you're never here these days."

She nods, understanding. "Yeah, well it's boy bonding night. Dane and Toby went camping."

I sit on the stool across from her as she washes the bowl.

"Then I say we should have girl's night out." I stand up.

"Where?" Ava asks, staring down at her yoga pants and T-shirt.

"I don't know. There's nothing to do in this town."

"I thought you'd be making Garrett dinner, you know your plan to show him what he's missing?" Her eyes light up with mischief like she's the one with the plan.

"Turns out I suck at that role." I shrug. "I've wanted Garrett for years, and I thought I had the patience and drive to slowly pull him out of the coffin he's buried himself in after Melissa died, but I don't. Is it so bad that I want him to chase me for once?"

She smiles and leans over the counter, placing both her hands on top of mine. "Not at all. Sometimes you need to show 'em what they're missing."

"And if he doesn't come to that realization?" I ask, fear twisting my stomach.

"Then he's stupid. But I've seen the way he looks at you, Charlie. I think you made the right move. Make him come to you."

I cross my fingers up in the air. "Here's hoping."

"What about girl's night in?" The back door opens at the exact moment Ava suggests that.

"Strike that," we say in unison and Vance stands confused in the doorway.

"Hello to you two, too." He heads to the fridge, grabbing a beer and cracking it open right away.

"Sorry, we were going to have girl's night in," I say and accept the beer he offers.

"I'm game. Are we gonna do face masks, eat chocolate, and talk about the boys we like?" He grabs another beer and sits down next to me, placing his chin in his palm, giving us his undivided attention.

I use my hand to push him off the chair and he loses his balance for a second but recovers quickly.

"I can bake something?" Ava offers and I laugh.

"You bake every day."

She shrugs. "I like it and Toby made me promise not to read any Harry Potter until he got back. He's having fun with us reading at the same pace and talking about it."

It's pretty cool how much Ava and Toby have bonded since she came into the Murray's life.

"Let's go play bingo." Vance slaps the table. "After we can go to Double D's and eat fries and burgers and milkshakes."

I crinkle my forehead trying to find my brother in there somewhere. "You really don't have much of a life in L.A., do you?"

"I'm definitely not playing bingo and eating greasy foods, so, humor me."

He stands up and holds out his hand for me.

I look over to Ava and she shakes her head. "I'm out. You two have fun."

What the hell?

I accept my brother's invitation and the two of us leave our beers on the counter and walk out the back door.

"See you two later," Ava singsongs right as the door shuts behind us.

Vance and I walk into the Veteran's Hall to play bingo, but Vance never makes it to the table. He gets stopped and asked a million questions about Los Angeles and what it's like being a big time producer.

In the meantime, I grab my bingo card and Miss Betty, the librarian lets me borrow one of her markers.

"You haven't been at Happy Daze very much," she says to me.

I nod. "I got a full-time job at the middle school, so, I don't need all the hours at the tavern anymore."

Her lips turn down. "Poor Dane. He'll be lost without you."

Miss Betty was in love with Marcus' dad. He died six years ago and I don't think she's moved on either. Not that there are a ton of prospects in Climax Cove. Especially for the over fifty crowd.

"He'll survive." I press my marker down on B four. "So, Miss Betty, any boyfriends?"

A slow rising smile turns up her lips. "No, Charlie. I'm not sure I'll go down that road again."

"Why not?"

She shrugs, pressing her marker on O seventy-two. She's one match away from bingo and I find myself hoping she wins. "I had the love of my life. I'll meet him in heaven when my time is up."

Great, another widower who says they can't move on.

I glance over my shoulder finding Vance stuck in the middle of four women from the Mystery Book Club asking him questions. He pleads with me to save him with his eyes, but I laugh and turn around. Serves him right for never visiting home.

"What about you? Rumors put you and Garrett Shaw together." Miss Betty waggles her eyebrows a few times.

"Rumors are wrong."

"Oh, I always thought you two would be wonderful together." She presses her marker on N thirty-four. "BIN-GO!" she screams and stands up, waving her card in her hand. She looks down at me. "You need to come every Saturday night. You're my good luck charm."

Fat chance.

I pick up my card.

"Congratulations, Miss Betty." I hug her and Mr. Lockheed walks over with the assistance of his cane to check her card.

With Miss Betty's winning cries fading, I stand outside the circle with Vance in the middle for a moment.

"Sorry, ladies, but Vance and I are heading to Double D's."

Vance gives me a thankful smile. We say our goodbyes and then head out.

"You're the best," he whispers when we're outside the doors.

"Okay, bingo is depressing. We're going straight to the French fries with chocolate ice cream," I say.

He swings his arms around my shoulders. "I have no idea how you do that, but tonight, it's on me."

It doesn't take us long to walk the block to Double D's and Vance opens the door like the gentleman my mom taught him to be, but my feet freeze when I get inside because the back and broad shoulders at the counter are way too familiar.

He never turns around and from what I can see, he's eating a slice of pie, drinking a coffee. Alone, in a diner on a Saturday night. Is this really what this man wants for the rest of his life? To live his life like he's already an eighty-year-old man?

"I was wondering when you were gonna come see me," Debbie says from behind the counter. The one-half of the Double D, runs over, wrapping her arms around Vance. "The big L.A. hotshot in the flesh." She steps back from their embrace and then slaps his shoulder. "Took you long enough to come home."

Garrett's chair spins around and I think the smile on his face must've been from expecting to see Vance because the corners tip down a bit when he notices me.

Vance rubs his arm. "Hey, Deb. Sorry," he mumbles.

"Come in, come in. Denis is out for the night, but we have a great night cook in that you'll love. What are you craving?" She ushers him to the booth.

My gaze follows them and I should be following, but a large body approaches me and I freeze. My voice catches in my throat.

"I need to talk to you," he mumbles and I look around.

Nope. Still just me standing here.

I guess we're doing this.

18

GARRETT

f I believed in it, I'd think fate sent her here to Double D's Diner.

When Deb went crazy with Vance's appearance, I couldn't help but smile, hoping she was with him.

I should've run after her when she left my house, but it took me a while to process my emotions. Always has.

Here she is, those toned legs still visible through the thin fabric of her leggings. A short skirt that hides her amazing ass and my favorite part of her body, her tits fitted snuggly secured in her shirt.

Vance is busy with Deb. She's now sitting down at the booth asking him if he's friends with George Clooney. Sometimes I've wondered if they're going to erect a statue of Vance for being some bigwig in L.A. The ones that want to flee from Climax Cove think of him as a God and the ones that prefer to stay here think L.A. is some magic bubble with celebrities around every corner. Then again, they could be right. I've only visited Vance twice and L.A. is drastically different than the small-town life of Climax Cove.

"No," she says in answer to my question.

She whips around, but I grab a hold of her elbow before she can escape fully.

"Please. It will explain a lot."

Charlie stares at me for a few seconds and then nods. "You can tell my brother." She leaves through the door and goes to wait by my truck.

Fuck.

I turn to Vance who is now sitting alone and watching the show between the two of us. He quirks an eyebrow up. A perfectly shaped eyebrow. Where is the guy who played rugby with me in the mud?

I trudge over, the knowledge that he might want to hit me again slowing me down.

"Hey."

"Why is my sister standing by your truck?" He never gets up from the table.

"I'm taking her to my house."

He scoffs. "The hell you are."

"We need to hash some things out."

He stares at me silently for a moment before responding. "You hurt her, Shaw. I saw it tonight." He taps his fork back and forth from tip to end on the table. One can only hope he isn't getting ready to stab me with it.

I nod.

"Tread carefully with my sister, man."

He eyes me and the seriousness in the eyes of one of my oldest friends isn't missed. Lucky for me, I have plans to make this all right.

"She'll be happy tomorrow, promise."

He holds up his hand and Deb drops a plate with a cheeseburger and fries on the table.

"No details, okay. I think I've been more than patient in

dealing with this thing with my sister, so don't make me regret it."

"Enjoy your cheeseburger." I grip his shoulder and try to convey as best I can that I have this covered.

I OPEN THE DOOR TO MY CABIN AFTER THE QUIET RIDE. I KNOW Charlie's mad because she's biting the inside of her cheek, which she does when she's bothered by something. It's a mannerism I've noticed when she's dealing with a rude customer at Happy Daze. She serves them with a smile and then gnaws on the inside of her cheek for awhile.

She walks through the door but lingers by the entry table as if she doesn't want to go any further.

"Have a seat on the couch. I'll be right back."

She sits on the brown leather couch and I head through the kitchen to my office.

The fact that I'm about to let Charlie see a side of me most don't has my heart hammering in my chest the entire way.

I open my desk drawer, find the paper I'm looking for laying where it always is. When I'm struggling, I read it. In the eight years I've had it, I've read it so often, I could probably recite it from memory.

Charlie is leaning on one side of the couch, her feet and legs tucked under her body. I place down the two beers I stopped to grab on the way here and she brings one of the bottles to her lips.

She eyes the paper in my hands, but says nothing, not recognizing it. Eight years is a long time and I don't even think she has any idea that I even knew about it.

"So, are we going to sit here all night in silence or are

you gonna tell me why I'm here?" her tone is short and bitter.

I cup the paper in my hand, shielding it from her eyes.

"You've liked me for a long time."

"No shit." She sips her beer again and places it on the table next to her.

"I've known it. I knew you had a crush on me when you were younger. As the years have gone by, I've noticed you looking at me differently than a young girl looks at her crush."

Her head falls to the side and those warm eyes now hold annoyance. "What are we doing here? Taking a trip down memory lane and going over what an idiot I am?"

I chuckle, but her lips remain tight.

"No," I answer.

Her chest rises and falls. "I'm about to call Al's Taxi and that should tell you how eager I am to leave here. He just had cataract surgery last week." She tips her beer in my direction and my dick stiffens, enjoying her snarky side.

"Relax. I'm getting to the point." Surprisingly, she does as I ask. "As you know first hand, after Melissa, I struggled with Sydney. I leaned on her parents and my own. Yeah, I was there physically to raise her, but I wasn't there emotionally. I fell into a deep depression."

Charlie puts her beer down on the table. "I know." Her tone is kinder now, which isn't the reason I'm telling her this.

"Sydney was four when my eyes opened the first time. It was the morning after your graduation party. Do you remember?"

She swallows and nods her head, her eyes steady on me now.

"I woke up the next morning and trudged up your

parents' basement stairs hung over to all hell. Sydney had gone home with my mom and I drank too much so as always, your parents took me in for the night."

I lick my lips and try to grasp a hold to every ounce of strength this piece of paper says I have.

"That morning, as your dad went out to get donuts for everyone and you and Vance were still sleeping, your mom sat me down at your kitchen table."

"My mom?" she asks, pointing to herself.

I nod. "She told me she understood my loss, but it was time to straighten up and take care of my responsibilities. That Sydney was essentially an orphan because I might be clothing her, feeding her, but I wasn't there emotionally for her. I wasn't participating in her life."

Her wide eyes tell me she's surprised, but I have no idea why since her mom isn't shy in conveying her feelings and thoughts. Like mother like daughter.

"We must've talked for an hour. Your dad came home, dropped the donuts on the table and then disappeared. I told her how I wasn't strong enough to be a single father. I wallowed in the fact that it wasn't supposed to end up this way. It was supposed to be both of us raising Sydney."

I inhale another calming breath. I think Mrs. Rose saw more of my raw emotions that morning than my own mother or even Melissa ever did.

"She gave me something that morning that made the difference. She may have crossed a line by giving me this." I hold the paper in the air. "Some might say it wasn't hers to give, but this paper right here helped me believe in myself again. Helped me find the man I was before tragedy struck. It helped me become the father I'm proud to be to Sydney."

"What is it?" Her voice is shaky and low.

I hand her the paper she wrote for her end of the year project in Advanced English her senior year.

She gasps and covers her mouth seeing the title, The World's Strongest Man by Charlotte Rose typed at the top.

"She didn't." She shakes her head and stands, rounding the back of the couch, starting to pace back and forth. "She told me she accidentally threw it away. The only reason she found out about it was—"

"Mr. Garfield wanted to send it into a contest."

She stops moving, her eyes tearing up.

"I told him no." She shakes her head, one tear slipping down her cheek.

"I know, your mom told me you refused and Mr. Garfield reached out to her."

She nods, her teeth nibbling on the inside of her cheek.

"It wasn't something you needed out there. I know how you hate having too much attention on you."

I stand, meeting her behind the couch. I reach up and caress her cheek, my thumb brushing away her tear.

"Thank you."

Her head shakes back and forth. "For what?"

"For always believing in me. For seeing something I didn't see in myself. You've always been my biggest cheerleader even if you didn't realize it."

She nods. "I'm embarrassed." She tries to turn her face away from me, but I grip it harder.

"Don't be. I should be the one who's embarrassed." My eyes focus on her warm and kind caramel eyes staring back at me.

"Why?"

"Because I shouldn't have made you wait, but I was so scared. In truth, I'm still scared." My gaze dips to her lips and back to her eyes.

"Don't be scared." Her hands reach up and cover mine. "I'm here for you."

I nod my head. "I want to explore what this is with you."

Her grin appears slow like honey flowing out of a jar until it paints every surface of her entire face with her happiness.

"Well try not to upset me again. That's strike one," she warns with a smile.

My head falls back and laughter pours out of me. "You really are a Rose aren't you?"

She shakes her head in confusion.

"Your brother is always logging strikes against me."

"I'm glad he isn't causing us too many problems."

The laughter slows and I stare into her eyes once more. What an idiot I was for not seeing what we could be sooner. "I'm going to kiss you now."

Her tongue snakes out of her mouth and I capture her lips before she can answer.

My body calms as soon as her lips are on mine, our tongues searching for one another's until they meet. I slow the kiss, but my lips continue to move along her jaw and down her neck.

"We have my house to ourselves tonight," I murmur against her soft skin.

"Then why do I still have clothes on?" Her hands hold my head to her neck and she steps closer to my body.

I pick her up and swing her over my shoulder, my hand sliding up her legs to her ass.

"Are you taking me to your cave?" she jokes, her own hands smacking my ass.

"I think I need to torture you with sweet kisses and tender words tonight."

She's silent and when I reach my room, I maneuver her

so she can slide down the front of my body. It's then I realize she's tearing up again.

"Why are you crying?" I ask and she shakes her head back and forth.

"I'm just happy."

I brush her tears away. "Then I hope to make you cry often."

She giggles, rising to her tiptoes and wrapping her arms around my neck. "Garrett," she whispers.

My hands flow over her body, feeling every inch of her. "Uh huh," I murmur.

"I still have clothes on," she says softly, her teeth taking my earlobe into her mouth.

I chuckle into her neck while my fingers reach for the zipper of her skirt.

19

CHARLIE

My skirt falls to the ground and Garrett's large hands slide under my leggings, pushing them down to join my skirt. Then his hands reach up and I raise my arms for him to take my shirt off.

"You're so beautiful." His rough beard doesn't itch or scratch, it's as though I'm home as his lips cascade down my belly, his hands leading the way as they hook on either side of my panties.

My center tightens when he slides the small piece of fabric down my legs and I step out of them. It's as though I'm not in my body as his hands glide along my skin and his lips come back up and he unclasps my bra letting it fall forward and down my arms.

In a snap of a finger, I'm standing naked in front of him.

My skin warms as I watch his gaze roam up and down my body, his tongue licking his lips, his eyes burning with desire.

"You have way too many clothes on." My fingers disappear under the hem of his T-shirt and he helps me by raising his arms. His chest is smooth with a sprinkle of hair that shows how much of a man he is. His muscles are hard, his abs tight and on display like I'm staring at the cover of a men's fitness magazine.

Flicking the button on his jeans, I carefully slide the zipper down, over the prominent bulge that makes my center pulse with anticipation. I push down his jeans and he steps out of them, and like that our clothes are mingled on the hardwood floor of his bedroom.

"Crawl on the bed," he instructs and there's something I like about him being bossy with me as if he's finally claiming *me.*

I slide down onto his green bedspread and scoot up the mattress.

"Just like that," he says, his eyes admiring the view of me spread eagle on his bed.

He drops his camo boxers on the floor and his hand strokes his large cock while he stares down at me.

"You are so gorgeous, Charlie."

Wetness pools between my legs while I watch him pump his dick with his eyes glued on me.

"You promised tender kisses and kind words." I smile.

"You're right, I did." His hand leaves his dick and they force my legs further apart.

Then he rises, nestling between my legs, as his hands brush my chaotic hair from my face and he captures my lips in a kiss that would weaken my legs if I wasn't already laying down.

"I want to lick you inch by inch, but at the same time I can't wait to be buried inside you again."

The tip of his dick is poised and ready at my entrance and I wiggle to entice him further. The wait is just as unbearable on my side.

"How about we save the mushy stuff for later?" I laugh

and he shakes his head, his hands sliding up my arms until my hands are clasp with his.

He circles his hips and then enters me slowly, inch by inch, my pussy begging for more until he's fully inside me.

"Garrett," I sigh.

"Shh...baby." His lips meet mine a few times. "We're taking this slow."

He grinds and I arch, my tits pressed into his hard chest.

"Oh," I moan and he thrusts again.

"You feel incredible."

I try to move my hands but he keeps them locked with his so that he has all the control except for my legs.

I plant the soles of my feet on the bed, widening my legs as far as they'll go so he can get as deep as we both want him.

"Jesus," he murmurs when he slowly drags himself from me and then thrusts in fast again.

My orgasm builds, all the blood flow centering between my legs and waiting for him to really start fucking me is an agonizing, torturous and somehow pleasurable endeavor.

"You're so wet," he whispers and I arch my body further, my fingers tightening around his.

He propels forward again and I wrap my legs around his torso, needing more of him. If we were velcroed together it wouldn't be close enough.

Our kisses become frantic and he releases my hands, holding my head in place while my fingers dig into his shoulder blades.

"Please Garrett, I need faster and deeper."

He growls but does as I request. His lips only leave mine for short breaths as he continues to grind in and out of me, his pace increasing, building my orgasm one step at a time up the steepest mountain.

My fingers clutch at him, the sweat between our bodies hindering my grip. Our mouths travel along each other's bodies in a chaotic mess.

He slows all his movements as his tongue gently slides into my mouth.

"Not yet. I want to see you come."

His hands brush the hair from my face and he stares into my eyes.

"Oh, Garrett," I sigh.

He says nothing, but his constant brushing of my mess of curls and the emotion in his eyes reveal his true feelings for me and pushes me off that mountain. He catches me with another surprise kiss like a parachute as I glide down back to earth in his arms.

His own thrusting slows and he circles inside me until his fingers tighten in the strands of my hair and he sprinkles open mouthed kisses along my jaw until he buries his head in my neck, gasping for air.

"Who knew slow sex could drain you too?" he chuckles into my throat and I wrap my arms around his neck, not wanting his body to leave mine.

"Yeah, and I haven't eaten since lunch."

He picks up his head, peering down at me as though I might be lying.

"Well then." He withdraws from me, disappearing into his bathroom, returning with a washcloth.

Once we're both cleaned up, he pulls on some boxers, throws me his T-shirt and then picks me up over his shoulder.

"Now to the kitchen," he says in what I imagine is his best Paul Bunyan voice.

I smack his butt. "If it's anything like the last time you cooked for me, I can't wait."

I'M PROPPED UP ON THE COUNTER, MY LEGS HANGING IN FRONT of me as Garrett moves between the stove and my legs. A taste of his chili followed by a taste of him every time he comes back to me.

"Cornbread in the oven. You've really embraced the single dad thing."

He rests the spoon next to the stove, locking me to the counter with his arms on either side of my hips. I wrap my legs around his waist and pull him into me further. My arms drape over his shoulders as he kisses the hollow of my neck.

"Can I ask you a question?"

He slides back, eyeing me. "Sure."

"Why now? I mean, what's changed?"

He stares down for a second and then meets my gaze with a seriousness that's been absent since he told me about the paper.

"When you walked out on me earlier, I realized I was more scared to lose you to someone else than to lose you completely."

I must look confused because he chuckles.

"I've shied away from you for a couple reasons. Your brother, your age, but most of all I was scared to put myself out there. I knew you were someone who could hurt me if I allowed myself to care any more for you than I already did and I never wanted to feel that despair again."

I tilt my head and run my hand down his rugged beard.

"But I have a confession," he says. A smirk appears on his lips and I smile a little, waiting for him to tell me.

"What?"

"I overheard you and Syd talking at the hospital. About her stressing that I'd be by myself when she goes away."

I draw back. "So this is to make Syd feel better?"

"No." He leans forward until my head gently hits the cabinets behind me. Garrett cups my face with his hand. "She asked you to wait for me."

I bite the inside of my cheek and nod, unable to look away from him.

"That's when I realized, I either lose you because of my own stupidity or I take the chance and never lose you. I read that paper you wrote again and I was reminded of the guy I was before it all."

"I've been seeing more of him these past few weeks." I smile.

"You pull that out of me."

My grin widens and I place my arms over his shoulders again. "Well, I don't want to brag." I flutter my eyelashes and he smashes his lips to mine.

Our kiss continues and our bodies drawing even closer. His hand slides up my bare thigh about to hit my center when the oven timer goes off.

"Tortured by the bell," I murmur against his lips.

"I'll be back in one second."

After he's taken the cornbread out and turned off the oven he slides me off the counter and onto his kitchen table.

I pull his dick out of his boxers and as the chili simmers and the cornbread cools, he takes me right there.

And the best part isn't the two orgasms he gives me. It's when he leans over me and says, "I haven't been this happy in a long time."

20

CHARLIE

My doorbell rings right as I put the last suitcase by the front door.

The smile on my face can't be denied when I open the door to Garrett standing on my doorstep.

I wrap my arms around his neck, and he backs me up into the apartment, shutting the door behind him.

"A whole day without you," he grumbles.

When my back is against the wall, his mouth descends on my neck.

"Too many clothes." His hands skate up underneath my sweater.

Thanksgiving was yesterday and since no one really knows we're officially a couple yet, we decided not to drop the news on Thanksgiving. Not that anyone will be upset. At least I don't think so.

"Well, the sooner we get out of here, the sooner these clothes come off." I giggle like the schoolgirl I've been around him since that night at his house.

He removes his hands from my body and grabs my bags. "Chop chop then, woman."

Then he disappears out the door.

We booked a long weekend with our group of friends up in the mountains.

I lock up my apartment and meet him at the truck. "So, Sydney was okay?"

"Yeah, she's happy to stay at Chloe's. Melissa's mom is going to pick her up Sunday morning." His eyes steady on me for a beat longer than they should, as though there's something he wants to tell me. Or maybe it's because Melissa's name came up.

"Great."

He shuts the tailgate and I move to round the back of the truck, but he grabs my hand and pulls me into him.

"You're just delaying your prize," I joke, but his face grows serious. "What?"

His legs widen and his strong hands grip my hips. "You've given me a new love of yoga pants."

I roll my eyes and shake my head. "I think you should use that mind to remember what I look like without yoga pants." I tap his temple and wiggle free, enticing him to start driving up to the mountains.

But he pulls me back and my hands hit his strong chest with an humph.

"You're scaring me, Garrett."

He shakes his head. "I want you to come to Melissa's parents on Sunday for dinner."

My mouth dries as he studies my face for some sort of reaction. Although my insides are working like an overwound clock, my outward appearance probably registers my surprise.

This is a big step. A step I wasn't sure he'd want to make this early in the game. I mean it's been a couple weeks that we've been together with no one truly knowing except

Sydney. Well, I'm fairly sure the guys know and I've told the girls, but the gossip mill in town doesn't. Hell, my parents don't.

"Um."

"If you don't want to, I understand, but I want them to know before they hear it from someone else."

I nod. "Okay."

The agreement might leave my lips, but my heart is still jackhammering in my chest, threatening to crack my ribcage in two.

He kisses my forehead. "You're the best. I had to get that out of the way so we can enjoy the weekend."

I'm glad he feels a little lighter. I would have preferred that bomb to be dropped Sunday.

Two hours later Garrett's truck is driving up the slick and steep hill to the mountain cabin. Luckily, my man has connections and got us all into a four-bedroom log cabin attached to Valley Ski Resort.

We pull up to the house and we're the first to arrive out of everyone.

"Perfect. Early bird gets the girl. Hurry." Garrett takes the keys out of the ignition and opens his door.

I'm still in my seatbelt when I hear the back tailgate open. The next thing I know, he's at my door with our two bags.

I unlock my seatbelt but before I have a chance to do anything else, my door is jarred open.

"You know Marcus is always on time. Let's go." He's ushering me out with his hand.

"What is the rush?"

"You and me naked before everyone gets here, that's the rush."

I laugh.

"We have our own room."

He shakes his head, linking my hand with his and dragging me out of the truck.

"I need your tits in my hands. I need my cock in your pussy and I need your screams in my mouth."

He closes my door, locks up the truck, and then we're trudging up the steps to a nice size log cabin.

"That was romantic," I remark, not that I truly care.

Garrett and I might struggle with making love over fucking, but he shows me his feelings in the ways that matter—like how he always feeds me after. The way his hands never leave me for very long. The way he can sit through an entire movie with me snuggled into his side and he doesn't even try to cop a feel. The way he has me text him when I get home if I leave late. The more time we spend together the more I see his old self is pushing through that dark exterior.

"I'll romance you tonight. Okay?"

I cock my eyebrow as he enters the code to unlock the cabin. He opens the door and then looks over at me, seeing my 'yeah right' expression.

He chuckles. "Yeah, probably not."

Grabbing both our bags, he throws them into the house and then picks me up like he always likes to do. Over the shoulder caveman style with his hand on my ass. The front door slams behind us.

He heads to the stairs, but I see my suitcase still there in the foyer, I figure this might be the best time to surprise him with my gift.

"Wait, grab my suitcase." I smack his back and he rears

back, barely bending and picking up my bag, leaving his. "Thanks," I mumble.

We peruse the upstairs, well, he does. I'm just along for the ride. He peeks into one room, and then moves to the next one and the next. I get the upside down view as my hair hangs over my head.

"Finally." We enter a room and from the king size bed and reading nook, I'm thinking he found the master bedroom.

Bringing me up, I slide down his chest, my hands stopping on either side of his face.

"Thanks for saving me the exercise."

"How about you repay me with a strip tease?" He winks and my insides go all gooey and soft.

"Sit down in the chair," I tell him.

He shuts the door and flicks the lock, toeing out of his shoes and stripping his jacket off on the way to the chair in the corner next to a bookcase.

"Bring it on, baby."

His arms are on each arm of the chair and the bulge in his jeans is already visible.

I unzip my jacket and toss it on a chest at the end of the bed. Taking the hem of my shirt in both my hands, I toy with him as I pull it up inch by inch, teasing him.

"Let me see your tits." He looks like he's about ready to leap up out of his chair and take over.

"You're a very bossy customer." I play the role of stripper servicing client and approval shines in his eyes. "But, since you're paying..." I strip my shirt off and drop it on the floor as I walk forward in my red satin bra and yoga pants.

"Forget the strip tease, let's go straight to you straddling me." He holds out his hands for me.

I bite my lower lip and shake my head, trying to portray my best sex kitten look.

Instead, I walk toward him, turn around and bend down as I pull my yoga pants past my ass, giving him a view of my matching red thong.

Smack.

I stand up and look over my shoulder secretly enjoying the stinging on my ass.

"No touching," I say wagging my finger back and forth like he's been a naughty boy.

His chest heaves and just to torture him a little more, I bend over and push my yoga pants completely off, after kicking my boots off.

Garrett kicks the ottoman that was in front of him to the side, widening his legs and holding his hands out to the side.

"Come."

I shift my jaw to the side and raise my eyebrows. "I think you said strip tease, not lap dance."

The you-got-me smile consumes his face and I can't hide my own grin from peeking out.

"What do I need to do for a lap dance?" he plays along, but my eyes flick to his hands undoing the button of his jeans and sliding down his zipper.

My two hands move to my back and unhook my bra, but I criss-cross my arms in front so it doesn't fall.

"Come on baby, let me see those tits."

"Ask nicely."

Once he pulls his cock out of his pants, my panties are drenched and the only thing I want to do is straddle him in that chair and let his big strong hands play with my tits.

"Please, Miss Rose."

"We switching the role playing up now?"

I drop my bra, not waiting for an answer.

His eyes widen and zoom in on my tits and I sashay as best I can over to him, pulling down my panties at the same time.

He holds out his hand for me, but instead of wrapping both my legs over his lap, I fall to my knees and fist his cock.

"Fuck," he groans, his head falling back to the chair.

Holding his dick up, I lick the underside until my entire mouth covers his tip and I swirl it around my mouth like a Popsicle.

His hands weave through my hair, tightening in my strands and holding me to him.

"Keep it up, baby."

My hand continues the pumping as I suck him in and out of my mouth.

"Damn."

A moan escapes my throat and I push down farther, trying to take him as far as I can handle. In past experiences, guys have tried to take control by pushing my head down, but Garrett's light touch on my head allows me to work at my own pace.

I continued to do the one sexual act I'm a little self-conscious about, but the small sounds leaking from Garrett's lips tells me I'm doing more than okay.

Unable to really cup his balls since we never took the time to relieve him of his pants, I deep throat him as far as I can once more and when the tip of his dick hits the back of my throat a full throttle growl ruptures from him, and his body shakes.

The pressure between my legs is unbearable. I reach down, my fingers sliding over my mound and I play with my clit.

"Shit, baby. I'm close," he warns, so I start working him faster.

He wanted my screams, but it's his pleasured noises that are filling the room. A few minutes later, he tries to push my mouth off his dick but I lock on to take him all in. I want to taste him.

Finally, he gives up on trying to stop me from swallowing and stills in my mouth.

I look up at him, my entire body on fire, impatiently begging for a release of its own.

He leans forward and picks me up under my arms and drops me onto the ottoman he kicked out of the way a second later.

Then it's him on his knees and my legs are spread open.

"I'm a tad worried about how well you sucked me off." He raises his eyebrows in question. "Don't tell me where you learned that from."

"Porn?" I joke.

"Perfect, we'll go with that." His finger slides up my center. "Now, let me show you what porn's taught me."

I laugh and his big palms lock my thighs down on the ottoman as his mouth descends between my legs.

I'm zipping up my pants, watching Charlie get dressed. She's gorgeous and although it's misogynistic because I enjoyed her efforts so much, I almost wish I had to teach her a thing or two about a good blow job. She worked me so fast, I was holding back my orgasm most of the time her mouth was on me.

"When are the others supposed to be here?" she asks, pulling her shirt over her chest and covering up some of her best assets.

"I'm surprised they aren't already. I'm sure Dane will be late, but Marcus? I thought they'd be here by now."

"Maybe Cat's having an effect on him." She pulls her hair back into a ponytail and puts her suitcase on the chest at the end of the bed.

I can't lie that being with Charlie has reminded me of Melissa. Not that Charlie is anything like Melissa, she's quite the opposite actually. Charlie is more carefree, makes jokes and lets a lot roll off her back. Growing closer to her has made me remember the only other time in my life that I had a woman in it.

It's moments like this when I question why I've gone without companionship all these years. Like the simple moments of spending the weekend in a cabin with our friends, or driving up here with her hand in mine as she sang to every song on the radio. Okay, I do need to introduce her to some of my favorite classic rock because one man can only listen to Justin Bieber songs so many times. It's the fact that tonight, I'll get to snuggle up behind her and hold her the entire time we sleep. I was stupid for waiting this long.

A box drops in my lap. "You seem pretty deep in thought."

I eye the box and then her as she situates herself on top of the mattress, with an expression that reminds me of Syd when she gives me my birthday gift—as though she wants to rip the paper away and open it all on her own.

"A gift?" I ask.

"Uh huh."

I shake the box. It's light and nothing except the shifting of something can be heard.

"Why?" I start to tear part of the wrapping paper away.

She leans forward. "I think it's time we upped your game in the undergarment selection."

"You don't like my boxers?" I ball the wrapping paper up.

"I like you out of them much more."

I grin and open up the box and there sits a pile of boxers. Starting with the top one, I pull it out. "You really into this role playing thing?" I hold up a red pair of boxers with a cross over the dick area and on the side, it says the doctor is in.

"Keep going." Her smirk tells me there's worse to come.

Boxers number two are blue and say "It ain't going to

suck itself" across the front. "Nice. I'll wear these later tonight."

She takes them out of my hands and hits me over the head with them.

"One more pair," she urges.

The third pair demonstrates just how off her rocker Charlie really is. It's a pair of boxer briefs with a spot for me to put my dick through. "You're kidding right?"

"Well, it can't pop out on you since the elephant nose fabric covers it all." She laughs, pulling the extra piece of long fabric out.

"Thanks?" I pose it more like a question.

"You're welcome. Oh and there are two other ones that are just regular boxer briefs." She leans forward, casting a small kiss on my lips.

"Does this mean, I get to do the same and buy you some underwear?" I put them in the box and toss it on the chair, pulling her to me.

"I have no objection to wearing new panties and bras that you pick out." With her back to me, I nuzzle my head into the crook of her neck. The scent of her perfume makes me hard as usual.

Then we hear a car pull up outside, ending the small amount of time we've had alone this weekend. I knew I should've booked us a separate cabin all our own.

DISHES CLATTER AND DANE'S VOICE BOOMS THROUGHOUT THE cabin. That serenity Charlie and I experienced hours ago would be nice right about now.

Charlie hops on my back and I carry her through the archway of the family room into the kitchen.

She lives for this crowd of people. Why wouldn't she? She's grown up in a huge family filled with aunts and uncles, cousins of all generations. Hell, I think she has a sixth cousin twice removed that still attends their Christmas events. No one is ever turned away from the Rose household.

Isn't that why she was so persistent with me? In a way, she couldn't leave me behind as everyone moved on with their lives and that's the reason she's attached to my back with her lips at my ear.

"Just a couple hours and then we'll pretend we're tired and go to bed," she whispers.

She knows me better than her brother, my best friend since preschool.

I nod.

"Look at you two, all cozy and affectionate." Dane points the wooden spoon at me.

Heat floats up to my cheeks and I'm thankful the beard helps shield my embarrassment from being called out. It's odd being with Charlie here in front of my friends. I'm just not sure why.

"Shut it, Dane," Charlie says behind me, dropping from my back as soon as we enter the room. She busies herself with Ava and Cat at the stove, the three starting to talk about the meal being prepared.

Marcus grabs two beers out of the fridge and nods out toward the deck.

I cringe from the cold, but I see the gas fire pit going. Sliding into my boots and shrugging on my coat, I join him.

He passes me a beer and says, "So, you did it huh?"

I nod, taking a sip.

"I'm proud of you." His smile confirms his words.

"I didn't just win the Nobel Peace Prize, calm the fuck down." I down another gulp. I hate all this touchy feely shit.

"No, but you conquered a fear." He leans forward and grips my shoulder, squeezing lightly.

I met Marcus shortly after he came to Climax Cove years ago, and we bonded over having daughters and no mothers. Although we might be cut from the same cloth in respect to the fact that we like control in our lives, he's way more comfortable with his emotions than me.

"I had to grab my balls and man up," I say with a shrug.

He chuckles, his eyes on the fire instead of me. "You'll be happy. Charlie's great and she seems like a great fit for you."

"I'm taking her to dinner on Sunday at Melissa's parents."

He's silent for a moment. "Really?"

I nod.

"Why so soon? I mean you guys just started dating, right?" There's no judgment in his voice, more curiosity.

"It'd be disrespectful for them to find out from anyone else. We've kept it quiet so far, but I'd like to take her out to dinner at some point." He clicks his bottle to mine.

"I like this new version of my friend much better." Marcus leans against the railing, what little we can see of the snow-covered mountains in the dark our only scenery.

The French doors open and out flows, Dane and Vance, with more beer in their hands.

"The ladies have it handled." Dane nods to the kitchen.

We all circle around the fire, silence descending down on us. It's odd without the kids joining us, but soon we fall into line and start chatting about the upcoming football games this weekend.

A half hour later, my balls are about to freeze off even with the fire pit and thankfully Charlie appears at the door to tell us that dinner is ready, her yoga pants outlining every curve of her body that I plan on licking later tonight.

The four of us go into the dining room where the girls have laid out the entire meal on the table.

"Man, I had no idea you could cook this well," Dane says, smelling the food on the table. "You've been hiding your skills from me." He points to Ava who smacks him over the head.

"Punishment is mine tonight." He waggles his eyebrows a few times letting everyone know at the table exactly what is about to transpire in their bedroom.

"Everyone sit down." Cat takes her seat next to Marcus, laying her paper napkin in her lap and sitting up straight.

"I feel like the fifth wheel," Vance says from across the table.

"You're actually the seventh wheel," Charlie corrects him and everyone at the table laughs.

"Tell us about L.A.," Ava says, her knife and fork poised over her chicken. "I've never been."

Dane glances over at her and then concentrates on his plate again. I swear maybe he was jealous for a minute there.

"It's nice, it's expensive, and like you'd expect is a 'who you know' kinda town. That's what is so great about Climax Cove. Everyone isn't constantly on the go and you can take people at face value."

"You enjoyed your bingo night then?" Dane asks and everyone laughs again.

"I did." Vance puts his fork in his mouth, smiling around it.

This kid bit at the first chance to get out of this town when he could and now he's saying how great it is to return? I don't buy it. Something's up.

"Do you know any celebrities?" Ava asks, her eyes lighting up with the possibility. Again, Dane's eyes shoot to her and then back to his dish. The green monster is definitely rattling his cage.

"Sure, I've worked with a few but then you get invited to a party and in walks Brad Pitt and George Clooney and you don't bat an eye. You get used to it." Vance cuts his chicken.

I lean back in my chair, my hand finding Charlie's leg under the table. She reaches behind me and her fingers run down the back of my head, playing with the ends of the longer strands on the top of my head.

"That's so fascinating. Who is the biggest celebrity you've met?" Ava's on the edge of her seat.

Who knew the girl was so celebrity crazy.

Vance looks up at the ceiling as though he's thinking. "I'd say Jack Nicholson? Yeah, I ran into him at a premiere. Coolest guy ever."

"Oh man, I'm jealous," she says.

I stifle a laugh.

So is Dane.

Vance has a smug grin on his face that says 'ain't my life grand?'

Dane's chair slides back on the floor. "Anyone need a beer?"

Ava stares up at him confused by the abrupt movement. "You okay, babe?" she asks.

"Just thirsty. No one else?" He tips his beer at each of us. "Just me? Okay."

He disappears back into the kitchen and Charlie's hand stops moving on the back of my head. When I look over, I find her gaze following Dane out of the room.

A seedling of jealousy sprouts in the pit of my stomach. Their close relationship has always bothered me. The way

Dane doesn't mind touching her. Yeah, yeah, it's in a sisterly way but he's not her brother.

She leans in close and I could say the words for her, because I know what she's going to say, "I'll be right back."

My hand falls off her leg and she stands, venturing into the kitchen after Dane.

I look up at the table and Ava's eyes are fixated on Charlie's back, her hand mindlessly grabbing her wine glass and chugging down half the contents before she re-joins the conversation.

A conversation about art. I get that Cat's an artist, but a day staring at paint on a canvas is not my idea of fun. Marcus is bragging about her, while Vance seems genuinely interested. Probably because his Twitter feed is one art gallery opening after another. I can only imagine his pretentious house in L.A. is filled with metal sculptures that resemble people having sex. Probably his version of foreplay with the women he brings home.

Okay, I might just be bitter that my girlfriend of only a few weeks just went into the kitchen with my best friend. It shouldn't bother me, I know I have nothing to worry about, but damn it my blood won't stop from heating.

Ava's gaze keeps flickering from the kitchen back to the table. Maybe I'm not the only one who's a little insecure about their newfound happiness?

A few minutes later, the two of them walk back in, Charlie with another bottle of wine and Dane with more beer. Ava grabs the bottle and refills her glass, downing half of it in a couple of gulps.

Yep. Someone has definitely lit the fuse on the stick of dynamite that is our little getaway with friends. Let's just hope it fizzles out rather than explodes.

The morning after our arrival I'm on the ski lift with Cat, when I spot Dane and Garrett already bombing down the hill. I was a little surprised when he said he wanted to split up the girls and guys today. Add on the fact he claimed he was too tired for any extra curricular activity last night in bed, and I'm fairly sure something is going on with my moody man.

"Does Garrett seem different?" I ask Cat.

She looks at me in her matching pink snow pants and parka and shrugs. "I don't really know. I mean he's usually quiet with me."

I bite the inside of my cheek. She's right. Garrett and Cat have never had to interact much together.

"Why?" she continues without me asking anything else. "Is there something going on?"

I shake my head. "I dunno. I just feel like he's pulled back a bit since dinner last night."

"Oh, I'm sure it's just the altitude. You know the air is thinner up here and maybe it's made him more tired. Some people have trouble adjusting." Her attention turns to

Marcus where he's waiting at the top of the ski lift. "He'll be tearing your clothes off tonight."

I nod and ski after her off the lift.

"I thought it was guys only," I remark, stopping to wait for Ava.

"They're all competing with each other. I'd rather ski with my snow bunny." Marcus kisses Cat.

I stick my gloved finger down my throat. "Seriously, Marcus, cheesy."

Cat laughs and leans on Marcus to hug him. "I'll be your snow bunny."

"Eww," Ava says, skiing right by us off the lift.

"Hold up." I ski toward her but she never slows down, and instead starts straight down the hill.

I glance back to find Marcus and Cat on the snow covered ground, Marcus trying to pull Cat up and her ski comes off. That's a hot mess I want no part of.

I chase Ava down the hill, but the girl is fast. Apparently her dad always takes her skiing during Christmas break ever since she was young.

Dane and Garrett are nowhere to be found, and when she reaches the bottom of the hill Ava begins skiing toward the lift immediately.

"Ava!" I scream.

She either ignores me or doesn't hear me, digging my poles into the ground with each stride, I ski as fast as I can.

By the time I get my butt on the chair lift, I'm one chair behind her and heaving for a breath.

"Ava!" My voice sounds like I have laryngitis.

Sweet Jesus, I need more physical activity in my life.

She glances over her shoulder but says nothing.

"I was trying to ski with you."

"Sorry, I'm more of a solo skier." She faces forward again.

I could call her on her bullshit right now, but instead I wait until we're at the top of the mountain.

Using all my power, I shuttle in front of her and stop. Cat and Marcus are just making it to the top cleft of the mountain. It seriously, took them this long?

"BABE!" Dane screams from a nearby chair lift heading up to the highest peak.

Ava and I both look up, finding him and Garrett side-by-side on a chair. Garrett never even looks at me. I'll admit—it stings.

"Meet me at the bottom of the double diamond to give me a celebratory kiss," Dane yells.

"What are the two of you doing?" I scream.

Dane's laugh bounces off every mountain tip around. I'm surprised he doesn't cause an avalanche. "Your boyfriend and I have a little competition going. Loser has to ski down the hill in his boxers."

Then their chair is moving past us and they're gone.

Garrett doesn't seem like the kinda guy to challenge another one so I don't get it.

When I look in front of me again Ava's gone and already started skiing down the mountain again.

"Ava." I catch her and keep pace but I really wish I'd bothered to notice that she went down a mogul ski run.

"Charlie, don't you get the hint? I don't want to talk."

Her body moves effortlessly up and down on each small hill.

"Why? Are you mad at me?" I weave in between them so I don't end up with a snow job for a facial.

"No...yes...I don't know. It's stupid."

My pace slows with her admittance and for the rest of the way down the slope, I rack my brain for a reason she'd be mad.

Once we're both at the bottom, I go to her side and we make our way to the bottom of the double diamond. "Ava, talk to me. What did I do to upset you?"

She huffs out a sigh. "It's stupid really which is why I didn't want to talk about it." She refuses to look at me so I patiently wait for more to flood out of her. "Your friendship with Dane...it's just so...close."

I bend over and laugh. "You're kidding, right?" When I look up at her, I see she's serious with her arms crossed over herself and her eyes focusing on anything but me.

"Ava." My laughter stops. "Dane is like my brother."

She nods, her eyes now shifting to the sky. "I know. Let's just forget it."

"Ava," I touch her arm but she still doesn't look at me. "I'm sorry if I did something."

"No, you didn't. I know how long you've known each other. I hate that I'm jealous of it. I think I'm just a little worried because we know Dane has the attention span of a squirrel and we've fallen into a routine lately. We don't have sex as often. We've been spending a lot of time with Toby. What if I become the old toy he doesn't want to play with anymore?"

"Oh Ava," I flip out of my skis and wrap my arms around her shoulders. "Let me tell you something. The other night, Dane came into the bar, giving me crap about Garrett and asking if his height is a reflection of his dick size."

Ava laughs, showing it takes a rare woman to handle Dane Murray's humor.

"Yeah, true Dane fashion. I asked him if his sex life was so dull he needed to imagine mine."

She smiles.

"He said he had more than sex. That when he went home, he got back rubs and cupcakes and the woman he's been waiting for all his life waiting for him." I raise my eyebrows and she turns away to hide her smile. "So, I'd say you have nothing to worry about."

She nods a few times and screams have us turning our heads toward the slope.

"They aren't?" I ask, my eyes glued to my new boyfriend skiing down the hill, his eyes on Dane.

"I think I may not be the only one who needs some reassurance." Ava looks at me and then to the two idiots on the slope.

"Not Garrett." I shake my head but Ava only purses her lips.

No way. She has to be wrong.

But when Garrett cuts off Dane, I'm worried she might be right.

I'm being a dick. And not just an average sized dick. A giant dick that hurts people when they fuck with him.

Dane's next to me on the ski lift, being a trooper and participating in every challenge I keep bringing up.

He's my best friend and I trust that he'd never be with Charlie, so, I'm confused as to why I'm treating him like a dog jumping through hoops and running up ladders.

Not only do I trust Dane, I trust Charlie. I never would've started dating her if I didn't, but when I see his hands on her, see them laugh together, I hate it.

If only my mind could convince my ego that we don't need to be skiing down a hill at warp speed and cutting off our best friend to beat him to the bottom of the hill.

I stop my skis at the end of the hill, happy as shit I beat Dane. Especially since I wore those damn boxers with the elephant trunk pouch my dick goes through.

"You're a moron." Charlie smacks me upside my head. "Did you think about Sydney when you were busy acting like a teenager?"

Her skis are off and her gloved hands are on her hips.

Dane laughs, skiing off to where Ava is waiting. Of course that bastard doesn't care.

"I was having fun," I say with a shrug.

"You were being macho and trying to prove something to yourself, you know that right? If you want to keep racing Dane then go ahead, but let's write a quick living will so we know who you want to take in Sydney after you're gone."

She stomps away toward where her skis are sticking up in the snow by Ava.

Since I still have my skis on it only takes me a few seconds to catch up.

"What was that all about?" I ask when I reach her.

She doesn't even turn to look at me. Instead, she takes her skis out of the snow, steps into them then uses her poles to propel her forward. Like the lovesick idiot I am, I follow behind her.

"Where are you guys going? I always follow through on my dares," Dane calls out, but at this point, I don't care.

"Talk to me right now," I say once I've caught up to her. Again.

She stops, slams her poles into the snow and lifts her goggles. "You talk. You're the loony toon who thinks I'd actually want Dane. Because yeah, Garrett, I pined away for you for years just to change course and go after your best friend once I have you." Her attitude is snarky and angry and my dick hardens under all the layers of clothes.

"Listen, I know it's irrational and I wish like hell I didn't feel like I had to prove myself, but you guys are close and I hate it when he touches you." My teeth clench and now my own poles are in the ground and I'm lifting my goggles to rest on top of my head.

"What the hell are you talking about? Am I being molested and don't know it?" Her eyes scan the area around her and then she covers her body with her hands. Sarcastic as always.

I wish it wasn't such a turn-on.

"You know what I mean. It's just Dane being Dane, still... the headlocks, the noogies, the way he sometimes has to touch your hip to slide behind you at the bar." My hands clench at my sides with every reminder of his hands on her body.

"You've been watching us?" she asks, the corners of her lips curling up.

"No." I shake my head.

She smacks me in the stomach. "You do so. You've watched me all this time?"

"No," I say the word, but my face loses the fight, and I roll my eyes the same way Syd has perfected. "A little."

"More than a little." She grins then steps out of her skis and rests them next to the fence we're near.

I wait for her to reach me, my heart beating and my palms clammy in my gloves.

"Admit it. You've been admiring all this time just like I have with you." Her arms wrap around my stomach and I'm still shaking my head no. "No?" she asks, and I know this is the last time she'll ask me before she walks away.

"What do you want me to say?"

"I want you to admit it. I want you to apologize for being a stupid caveman and putting your life in danger in some crazy competition of male machoism."

Her arms are still wrapped around me and even with our layers upon layers of clothes my body heats with her nearness.

"And if I admit it?"

"We'll go back to the cabin and I'll show you exactly why you have nothing to worry about."

I blow out a breath, not used to putting myself out there this much. "Fine. Yes, I've watched you for a long time and I don't like the way Dane thinks he can put his hands on you. You're mine now and I don't want to act like a Neanderthal, but I don't want anyone else touching you."

She smiles wider now, backing away from me. And then she turns around and positions her skis so she can step into them again. When I don't immediately follow, she glances over her shoulder, a flirtatious smile on her beautiful face. "Are you coming?" she asks in a tone an octave lower that tells me good things are coming my way.

"Hell yeah." I follow her until we're near the exit and we hear an outpouring of laughter coming from behind us.

We look to where the voices are and low and behold there's Dane, skiing down the double black diamond in a pair of thong panties.

"Should I cover my eyes?" Charlie kids next to me.

"Now that I see what he's working with, I feel much better."

Charlie laughs and we race each other back to the cabin.

I should open up more often if this is always going to be the payback.

My back crashes down onto the bed and Charlie falls on top of me.

"Are you convinced?" She stares up at me with her chin resting on her hands on my stomach.

"Yep, we're solid now."

She slides to my side and I cradle her in my arm as her fingers run up and down my chest, playing with the small amount of chest hair I have.

"Now that the whole jealousy thing is out of the way, I think it's safe to say we both feel strongly about one another." There's some hesitancy in her voice.

I pull her closer and kiss the top of her head. "I think it's safe to say that."

"Then can I ask you a question in the interest of full disclosure?"

My stomach clenches so tight, you'd think I ate a five-hour-old hot dog at the convenience store.

She sits up, grabbing a hold of my shirt on the edge of the bed and tossing it over her head.

"We don't need to get dressed. I'm sure Dane's in a cell somewhere."

Usually she'd laugh, but this time she doesn't. Instead, she crosses her legs and plays with the hem of my shirt.

"Charlie, what's on your mind?" I ask, sliding up to rest my back against the headboard.

"We never really talked about the vasectomy thing."

I blink a couple of times. Of all the things I thought she'd say, this wasn't it.

"Okay..."

"Do you not want to have any more kids?"

Funny all these weeks we've been together this topic didn't even surface in my mind, but I can see now that she's been giving it some thought and that she might have a problem.

Before I can even respond she starts rattling on...

"I mean, I *do* want to have kids some day. I understand why you might not, and I'm totally cool with adoption or a sperm bank or something, but I don't see my future without them. And if we're getting more serious—"

I press my finger to her rambling lips.

"I understand that you want to have kids. Hell, I'd have ten more Sydney's."

She's still focused on the hem of my shirt as she folds it and fists it within her fingers.

"When I got a vasectomy, it was out of self-preservation. I wanted to make sure what happened to me with Melissa wouldn't happen again. It was a hasty decision. But if this goes further and we reach that point in our relationship, I'm definitely up for us having kids. Adoption sounds awesome."

She grins and I dip my head to see hers. "So, you're willing to have more kids if we work out?"

I laugh. "Yeah, I am. I love being a dad, Charlie and I think you'll make a great mom."

I don't bother to question why I'm not freaked out about having this conversation with her. I guess on some level I knew I'd have to have it with any woman I was serious with.

"Oh, I'm so happy! I had no idea how to bring that up to you." She tackles me to the bed and sprinkles my face with kisses. "Thanks for being a jealous idiot."

I tilt my head. "Am I supposed to say you're welcome?"

Her hand slides down my body and she fists my already hard cock.

"Ready for round two? Especially after you froze me out last night?" She shakes her head at my jealous idiocy.

I flip her over and she squeals. "I have nowhere I'd rather be."

THE NEXT MORNING, I SNEAK OUT OF THE BEDROOM TO GRAB some food to bring up to Charlie. I'm walking down the open hallway on the second story, which allows me to see the entire downstairs.

Vance is in a pair of low slung pajama pants at the door lip-locked with a blonde. I wondered what happened to him yesterday. Mystery solved.

Trying to not be noticed, I quietly walk into the kitchen and open the fridge and grab the carton of eggs.

"Hey." Dane opens up the French doors from the patio and I jump. The carton of eggs drops from my hands and cracks echoes through the cabin.

"Jesus, man."

"You broke all the eggs."

I pick up the eggs and open them up, finding none salvageable.

"Only because *you* surprised *me*." I dump them in the trashcan. "Guess we're going out for breakfast."

"Ava and I are heading out early today since you hogged all my time yesterday." He sits down at the kitchen table.

"Sorry about that." I fill a cup of coffee and lean on the counter behind me.

"We good?" he asks and from his somber tone he knows exactly what was up with me yesterday.

"Yeah, we're good."

He smiles and I remember him skiing down the hill in a pair of thong underwear.

"I can't believe you followed through on the bet."

He stands pushing in his chair. "I always pay my debts. Now, I talked with Ava and I know you said we're good, but I want you to know, I understand. I wouldn't want you touching my girl, so," he raises his hands in the air. "These will stay in my pockets from now on."

"Thanks." I could say it doesn't bother me as much anymore now that Charlie and I have discussed it, that I feel secure in our relationship, but truth is, I'm accepting of my caveman status and I don't want him touching her.

I don't want *anyone* else touching what's finally mine.

Garrett's hand rubs up and down on my thigh because he wants the anxiety attack that's teetering in my body to calm.

A two-hour drive home from the best weekend of my life has had my emotions swirling like a unicorn's horn and I'm desperate to calm down before we reach Melissa's parents' house.

"You know them." He squeezes my knee. "They know you."

Boys are such clueless creatures.

"They might think I'm too young or—"

"Shh." He shakes his head. "They already know about you, and they are okay with me moving on."

I nod my head like a damn bobblehead trying to convince myself they aren't going to go all Benson on me and give me the third degree when I get there.

Maybe I've been watching too much Law & Order lately.

Garrett's right, I know Phil and Violet. Not terribly well, but enough that'd we exchange pleasantries if we saw one another on the street. Violet threw herself into mothering Sydney right after Melissa passed and I don't blame her.

"So, Sydney's close to them?"

Stupid question, Charlie. I have this annoying habit of needing to fill the silence when I'm nervous.

"Well, they are her grandparents, but I'll admit that their relationship is changing with Sydney growing up. Trips to the candy and toy stores are no longer the way to Sydney's heart. Violet is struggling a little, but she asks Sydney's help with how to work social media to try to stay connected."

I pull out my phone, laughing. "Violet is on Facebook?"

"Not only Facebook, but she's got an Instagram and she's been asking Sydney about Snapchat." He looks at me from the corner of his eye.

"Who are her friends?"

I find her account. A nice picture of her and Phil on a cruise is set as her profile picture.

"Sydney."

We laugh and the truck seems a little less stifling.

GARRETT PARKS ON THE STREET IN FRONT OF A NICE LOG CABIN style house in Wet Rock.

"Did you build this for them?"

The architecture looks very similar to his other ones.

"They used my same architect and I had my crew do most of the work."

We exit the truck and this immediately feels like the most awkward situation I've ever been in.

"I should have brought something different to wear." I pull my sweater down as far as it can to cover my leggings.

"Don't be silly. I love these things you wear." His hand slides down my back to my ass and he squeezes it.

"Nope." I circle out of his hold. "No touching."

"No touching?" he questions. "That's not what you said last night."

"I'm serious, Garrett. No wandering hands under the table." I point to him and he crosses his heart with his finger, but the smirk on his face says I can't trust him one bit.

"Here we go." I mumble as we walk up the paved walkway, Garrett in front of me, leading the way. "What a cute goose." I pat its head. It's so cute all dressed in a turkey outfit.

"I'm surprised he isn't changed into Santa yet." Garrett looks at it with an exasperated expression and I laugh.

"I think you should get one."

He rings the doorbell and I try to distract myself with the goose.

"A big one for you and a small one for Sydney. I think Georgette Heinemann makes their clothes. At least she had a craft booth at the last festival with a bunch of these."

His hand lands in mine and his free hand brushes against my cheek.

"Relax, baby."

I quiet and pretend I'm not hyperventilating inside.

The door opens and Violet smiles, her hair much grayer than I remember. She's wearing jeans and a knit sweater that says, Bring on the Merry Balls, with giant ornaments adorned to the front.

"Charlie." Her arms outstretch.

Okay, we can pretend this isn't awkward. We can act like we're best buddies.

"Hi, Mrs. Bender."

She doesn't squeeze hard and our bodies barely touch, but it's a nice gesture.

"Please, call me Violet." We separate and I catch Sydney on the couch in front of the television inside. Shouldn't this be a big thing to her, too?

"I'm so happy you both could join us for dinner." She ushers us in and I might have entered a time warp from twelve years ago.

Pictures of Melissa from birth to what looks like just before she died are hung on every wall. Her in gymnastics, her in girl scouts, and her as a cheerleader. I can't help the feeling that her eyes are staring at me, judging why I'm here.

Garrett's hand slides in mine and he pulls me toward the family room.

"Hey, Syd. Did you have a good weekend?" Garrett asks her and he sits us down on the couch.

I cross my legs, trying to concentrate on everything but the giant water-colored portrait of Melissa when she was in her teens.

"Not as fun as skiing." She glances to her side at us both.

"I told you, we'll plan something during Christmas break. This was a couples thing." He places his hand on my knee and squeezes.

"So, Charlie, how is that brother of yours? Vance? I heard he's a big movie producer or something in California." Violet joins us in the family room and I slide a good foot away from Garrett.

She drops a tray of veggies and dip and those hot dogs wrapped in dough on the table.

"He's actually back in Climax Cove at the moment," I say.

Garrett closes the distance between us, reaching over my

lap to grab an appetizer. I'm not sure the man ever saw food he didn't like.

"Oh, I'm surprised the Climax Cove gossip hasn't hit me out here yet." She sits in the chair opposite us. "Sydney, let's turn off the television," she says in a nice voice that sounds like she's giving her granddaughter the option.

Sydney does as she's asked but just replaces it with her phone.

Mr. Bender enters the room with a beer for Garrett.

"Thanks, Phil." He's so at ease around them and the shrines of Melissa on every surface.

"Hi, Charlie." He nods, a folded piece of paper under his arm and a pen above his ear.

"Hi. Mr. Bender." I raise my hand in a small wave.

"Phil." He stares down at me over the rim of his reading glasses. "Can I get you something to drink?"

Violet stands. "I'll get it. I bought us a special bottle of wine." She winks and then disappears into the kitchen.

She's going to poison me.

Garrett knocks his elbow into me lightly and I give him a tight smile in return.

She's going to poison me.

Maybe if I think it hard enough, we'll telepathically communicate and he'll save me from certain death.

"Charlie, do you like white?" Violet returns with two glasses.

She stops on the other side of the coffee table and I kindly reach for a glass, but she moves it away from me and then gives me the other one.

"Oh, wait." She stares at them for a minute. "Okay, here you go." She hands it to me and I grip it not really wanting to take a sip. "I took a small taste in there and I've felt off all day. I wouldn't want you to get sick." She smiles, sitting in the chair and crossing her legs.

Not sick. Dead.

"Thank you." I place it on the table.

"Taste it and let me know what you think? There's a new winery my friend's son opened. It's from there."

All eyes move to me, well, only Garrett and Violet's. Sydney's are stuck on her phone, and Phil's are on what I think is a crossword puzzle.

Looking at Garrett, I memorize his face.

It's been a nice life I think to myself and then take a tentative sip.

It's crisp and fresh. "Very good."

"I know, I might splurge and buy a case." She cringes like it's the most absurd thing in the world. "You two should go there sometime."

I nod and look over to Garrett who is busy chomping down on his fifth carrot.

"Okay, Syd," Phil says and Sydney picks up her head to look at her grandpa. "Temporary cessation of breathing."

Sydney's thumbs start moving on her phone and a second later, she mumbles, "Apnea."

"Yes." Phil's eyes widen and he writes in the answers. "Always so good at these." He smiles but never looks up.

Sydney sneaks a glance at me and Garrett shakes his head, smiling to himself.

"This is a hard one. Egyptian fertility god."

Again, Sydney's thumbs move across the phone and Phil's head remains down.

"What does it start with?" Sydney asks, a Cheshire smile on her lips.

"Um..." Phil's eyes scan the page. "A and it's four letters."

"Could it be Amon?" Sydney asks like she's not staring at the answer on Google.

I shake my head, but when I turn I find Violet's eyes on me. She's not smiling, but she's not frowning.

Once she notices I'm looking her way, her lips curl up into a small grin.

Is she waiting for the effects of the poison to set in?

"Let's eat before Garrett fills up on appetizers," she says.

I look down at the plate seeing most of it gone and look at him.

"Hey." He tilts his head. "I had a nice workout this weekend," he mumbles and I hit him in the stomach, making him laugh loud enough that the other three people in the room turn our way to investigate what's so funny.

"What did you make, Violet?" Garrett asks.

Again, Garrett takes my hand and although I'm slightly uncomfortable with the whole scenario, I'm thankful to have his strength to lean on. Especially knowing how hard this must be for him.

"Meatloaf, your favorite. You're not a vegetarian are you Charlie?" her voice softens the further she disappears into the kitchen.

"No, Charlie loves meat. You should see how she mows down on it," Garrett answers for me and I hit him in the stomach again.

We sit down at the table beside each other with Sydney sitting across from us.

He leans in close to me and lowers his voice. "Keep doing that and they'll think you abuse me."

I shoot him an exhausted expression.

"Oh, good." Violet comes in with meatloaf. "I was worried since I keep reading about all these young kids not eating meat and if they do it has to be grass fed or something."

"No, I'm still a carnivore." She looks down from where she's standing next to me and again that small smile forms. I have no idea if it's real or fake.

The five of us sit down and start to pass around the dishes. Phil continues to do his crossword puzzle and Sydney answers his questions with her phone without him knowing. Violet seems set on asking me about every person in town since she doesn't get back to Climax Cove as often as she'd like, but I think it might have more to do with the memories that flood her mind when she crosses the city sign. I feel for Violet and Phil, I truly do.

Once dinner is done, Violet starts clearing the dishes.

I scoot my chair out to help. "Oh no Charlie, you're a guest." Violet shoos me to sit back down, but where I grow up that doesn't matter.

"Why should you do all the work? If we work together, we'll get it done faster." I eye Garrett, who sits there, his arm resting on the back of my chair and looking like he might take a nap from the food coma he's in.

I kick the foot of his chair and he startles.

"We'll all help." I eye his plate and then the kitchen doorway.

He scrunches his up his forehead.

"Sydney," I call to her and she looks at me like I morphed into an alien. "Get your plate and take it into the kitchen."

Garrett and Sydney pick up their plates and do as I ask. Violet is already rinsing some of the dishes when we enter.

"We'll wash and dry. The two of you clear the table."

Violet washes and I dry, stacking the dishes on the kitchen counter.

Garrett and Sydney don't argue as they come and go, placing the dirty dishes next to Violet. Garrett even places the salad dressing back in the fridge and throws away the dirty napkins.

"Table is clear." Garrett comes up to me.

"Okay, we're almost done." I smile at Violet.

"I have dessert in the fridge. Strawberry Jell-O custard trifle," Violet says.

"Garrett." I nod toward the fridge.

For a man who does everything he does, he sure lets Violet cater to him.

"Oh, I'll get it." He smiles at me.

I find some paper plates in the cabinet as I'm putting away the dishes in the cabinet Violet directed me to.

"Let's use these and then we have fewer dishes." I smile.

"Good idea, and I have some plastic forks too." She rushes over to a butler pantry, digging through the bottom until she lifts a box out. "Got them."

Afterward, we eat dessert and then it's time to go. All in all, it wasn't near as bad as I'd predicted.

"Bye, Grandma," Sydney says, hugging her much shorter grandma. It's clear that Sydney's inherited some of Garrett's height. "Grandpa." She shifts to give Phil a quick hug.

"We'll see you soon," Violet says.

Garrett kisses Violet on the cheek and then Phil shakes his hand. They wait for me on the porch, Sydney patting the goose's head.

"Garrett honey," Violet says as we all step out onto the porch. "Before you go, can you and Sydney get the canopy down from the garage? We're having friends over next weekend and I don't want Phil to hurt himself," Violet asks sweetly.

"Sure." Garrett looks at me and I step up to say my good-byes, thinking I'll help them.

"Charlie, can we have a quick word?" Violet asks and Phil blows out a breath.

Okay, she's going to tell me the poison will hit in a few hours.

"Sure," I say.

Garrett and Sydney both head around the side of the house, chatting as they go.

I'm still looking in their direction when Violet grips my hand. "Phil and I just wanted to say thank you. We know Garrett and Sydney's situation isn't easy, that this dinner wasn't easy, but we want Sydney to have a mother figure in her life and Garrett deserves to be happy. We had reservations about you because of your age, and I can't speak for Phil, but you're perfect. It's clear you two love each other." She hugs me and this time she presses so hard it's difficult to breathe until she holds me out by my upper arms. "I hope that there will be room for Phil and me in your lives together."

Did I miss Garrett's proposal? I know I can zone out, but I'm fairly sure I'd remember him down on bended knee.

"No worries there, Violet." She squeezes my arms and then releases me so fast, I back into Phil.

"Sorry," I mumble, gaining my footing.

Looking to the side of the house they disappeared behind, I wonder what is taking Garrett and Sydney so long.

"Bye, Phil. I don't know how you'll do those crossword puzzles without Sydney." I raise my eyebrows in question.

He chuckles. "You gotta find a way to relate to your growing granddaughter somehow. Am I right?"

"Yeah." I nod. "Thank you," I say to both of them and then walk down the front steps, seeing Garrett and Sydney emerging from the side of the house.

We all climb into his truck and wave goodbye to them as they wait on the porch for us to pull away.

"See, not that bad." Garrett reaches over and squeezes my knee.

"No, not bad."

"You were worried, Charlie?" Sydney asks from the back seat.

"A little." My phone dings in the cup holder and I pull it out.

"Looks like Violet Bender follows two people on Instagram now." I hold my phone up to Garrett and Sydney showing them my new follower.

We all laugh and my heart warms thinking I have everything I could truly ever want.

25

GARRETT

Christmas is in five days and I might be exhausted, but the family cabin for the Banks family is finally complete.

The three of us drive up to welcome them. When we arrive Sydney grabs the bag of groceries I include with all my rentals.

Jasper Banks and his wife, Lennon, have been one of my biggest and most loyal clients, so I've gone one step further with my welcome for them.

I've included a basket with everything from our local shops—an assortment of cupcakes and cookies from Mad Batter, coffee coupons from Steaming Hotties, and other samples or small trinkets from other shops downtown. Each bathroom will have a new soap from the newest shop in Climax Cove called Some Like It Slippery.

"I'm loving the Winter Pine scent of this soap from the new shop." Charlie smells it, grabbing the box of soaps to place all over the house.

We open up the doors and Charlie and Sydney both gasp and look at one another.

"Dad," Syd walks in, her eyes wide, looking all around.

"You've outdone yourself." Charlie looks back at me with a proud smile on her face.

"It was a lot of work, but it turned out how I wanted." I grab the bag from Syd and head to the kitchen, putting the items away.

"Will you build me one?" Charlie asks, dropping the box of soaps on the granite counter in the open concept kitchen.

"There's a pool table and one of those games with the little men on sticks!" Sydney calls out and I can tell she's impressed. Sydney being impressed is a hard accomplishment these days so I smile as I'm adding the last of the items in the fridge.

"And a hot tub and a pool." Charlie sounds as excited as my daughter.

"And a theatre room," Sydney yells from deep in the house.

"And brown leather couches." They both say in unison and then look at each other and laugh.

"Always brown," Syd says.

"Always leather," Charlie chimes in and she touches Sydney's shoulders as they both bend at the waist laughing.

"It's rustic, okay," I add on but I'm not even sure if they hear me.

"Let's go upstairs." Charlie grabs the box of soaps from the counter.

Their footsteps move from one bedroom to the other all I can hear are their ohhs and ahhs.

"A whirlpool tub." Charlie's voice sounds envious.

"In three of six bedrooms," Sydney says.

"Hey, I have four extra soaps," Charlie says from the banister above me.

"There are rooms in the lower level, too," I remark, folding the paper bag from the store.

"There's a lower level?" Sydney asks and starts running down the stairs, her socks making her slide a bit but she catches herself on the railings.

"Wait for me." Charlie moves slower but just as eager to see the rest of the house.

"Oh. My. God," Sydney screams.

Ten minutes later, they come up with an empty box, shaking their heads in disbelief.

"Garrett, it's gorgeous."

"Yeah, Dad, like top of the line. They're going to love it."

Charlie places the box on the counter next to the cupcake display. "So, you want me to build you one?" I ask since she mentioned it jokingly earlier. We haven't really talked about our long-term plans, but I miss her when she works late and sleeps at her apartment. I haven't broached the subject with Sydney yet, but I think I want Charlie to move in with us.

She wraps her arms around my waist and stares up at me. "Not this big, but yeah, maybe someday, we can build one and make it ours."

I smile and nod, my mind already overflowing with ideas on how I'd work with Ian, my architect, in order to make it ours together.

Sydney acts like she's on her phone and isn't paying attention but I know she is. One thing I learned early on with her is that even if you think she's in her own little world, she's *always* listening. I'm hopeful that her silence is an agreement that Charlie should move in with us.

The doorbell rings and then a knock sounds out and then the doorbell and then another knock on the door.

"Oh man," Charlie murmurs and her and Sydney share a wide-eyed look.

I slide out of my embrace with my girl and walk up the two steps to the front door.

The doorbell rings again, And again and again.

I open the door to two small kids. The boy's fist is in the air now ready to knock and the girl's finger is on the bell.

Looking out to the driveway, Jasper and his wife, Lennon are taking their suitcases out of the SUV.

"Hey, Banks!" I holler out with a wave.

Jasper waves and then looks over to Lennon. They share a confused look.

"Sorry about our little hellions. They're just excited," Lennon calls over, her dark hair a bit longer than the last time I saw her.

"Is that them?" Charlie peers under my arm. "The sex toy developer?" she whispers, but I don't know why because the two kids just ran into the house.

"Nice truck." Sydney walks to the door, her eyes on their expensive SUV. I'm guessing that Sydney isn't going to be a Climax Cove lifer based on her love of material things and money.

"Let's go, Brady," Jasper yells into the truck and the back door opens.

"That's the older son," I say about the brown-haired boy who's grown inches since I saw him last.

He's in basketball shorts and a T-shirt with headphones resting on his temples. Did someone forget to tell him it's December?

"What's his name?" Sydney asks and both Charlie and I turn our heads in her direction.

"His name is Stay Away."

Charlie laughs beside me, looping her arm with Sydney's while I head over to the vehicle to help them out.

"Hey, Garrett," Jasper tries to put his hand out but between the small backpacks and suitcases, there's no room.

"Later." I grab items from the back of the truck.

"Thanks. Who knew we'd have to come with so much?" Lennon shakes her head, her tattoos hidden under the warmth of her jacket. Good thing. I don't want Sydney getting any ideas. Right now, I'm pretty sure she just thinks it's her dad and his friends who sport the things.

"That's what happens with kids, right?" I understand although I only have one and if she has her phone, we don't have to worry about much else these days.

"Wow. It's amazing, Garrett." Lennon looks up as we're walking toward the porch and takes in the big family cabin and even I'm impressed with how immaculate it looks with all the lights lit up. "Who's the brunette?" Her tone comes with accusations.

"Charlie."

She stops and raises her perfectly arched eyebrows. "Is Charlie special?"

I chuckle but don't answer.

She elbows me in the ribs and I almost drop the bag filled with marshmallows, graham crackers, and chocolate. "Tell me."

"Yeah...she's special."

"Oh, I love it." Her footsteps pick up speed.

Jasper leans in close. "You should've pleaded the fifth on that one. Not that she'd have accepted that as an answer anyway."

We both chuckle at his cordial way of saying his wife can be persistent.

"You have got to be shittin' me!" Lennon's screams and drops her bags in front of the door.

"Babe!" Jasper hollers to her back as she walks into the cabin, ignoring the discarded items.

"Here." Charlie bends down and slides them to the side.

"Thanks. I'm Jasper."

"Charlie." She smiles that one that lights up her face.

Just then their two little ones run down the stairs. "Mommy, I found my bedroom," the little girl who, if I remember correctly, is Bianca says.

Lennon pats her on the head. "You two are sharing with your cousins. I think there's a big room at the end of the hall with a lot of bunk beds." Lennon looks over their heads to me.

"Yes, there is," Charlie answers first.

Lennon points to Charlie. "Charlie. I'm sorry. I get kind of excited when I come here. Jasper brought me up here when we were first dating and it's nostalgic for me." She looks over at her husband and he shakes his head because he knows how emotional she gets.

"I'm Lennon Banks." She holds out her hand. "Oh, jeez, forget the polite hand shake. That's what I just did all week in meetings." She holds out her arms. "Bring it in. Give me a hug."

Charlie steps in and Lennon wraps her arms around Charlie and they move side to side.

"I'm so damn happy that Garrett has found someone."

"I'm happy it was me." Charlie shrugs after Lennon lets go.

Lennon's eyes go wide. "Cupcakes?" She slides past Jasper over to the counter, picks one up, and takes a bite. "Holy fudge buckets you have to try one of these, babe. You know what would go well with this?" She eyes her husband.

"Coffee?" he deadpans.

"I left it in the truck." She shoots him please and thank you eyes and Jasper walks out of the cabin shaking his head.

"Mommy!" The little girl screams down from the banister.

"Bianca, stop screaming!" Lennon yells back. "Keep the crazy contained until we're alone."

The little girl runs down the stairs and climbs up on the chair. "Cupcakes?" Her eyes bulge and Lennon hands her a white one.

"Not taking my chances in this place. No chocolate and no colored drinks." She looks at Charlie and nods as though she'd understand.

Bianca takes a bite and then the little boy comes out of the game room.

"They have a pool table." He holds the eight ball in his hand.

My whole body stiffens as I imagine the four-year-old tossing the pool ball around like it's a toy.

"Give me, Evan," Lennon holds out her hand.

"No fun." He climbs next to his twin sister and grabs the chocolate cupcake.

"Nope. No. Only outside." She exchanges it with a vanilla. "And don't leave those stools until I wipe your hands and faces." She points to them and then walks toward us.

"Evan, Mommy said don't move," Bianca repeats and Evan takes his fingers and smashes it into the cake. "Evan, Mommy said."

Evan puts his hand to Bianca's face. Bianca takes the hand and makes him hit himself. She laughs and Evan narrows his eyes.

Missing the whole display behind her, Lennon approaches us. "Thank you so much, Garrett. My family is coming up tomorrow and that's crazy town." She directs her attention to Charlie. "I know what you're thinking, crazier than this, but if you come back tomorrow, us five will look like the Cleavers." She laughs and I catch her tattooed finger with a J on it.

"I come from a big Italian family, so I get it," Charlie says.

Lennon waves her hand and then wraps her arm around Charlie. "You totally get it then, but having kids brings things to a new level of insanity."

"There she goes again," Bianca says to Evan who's busy dipping his fingers into each cupcake.

"In a good way. I'm not saying anything bad, Bianca." Lennon shakes her head.

"I believe you, Mommy." She follows that line with a roll of her lines and I hold back a chuckle."

"Just eat your cupcake." Lennon's voice raises an octave.

"Where's Sydney?" I look around not finding her anywhere.

"Brady's missing too." Lennon does the same. "Uh oh, I wonder if there's been a love connection. Someone call Chuck Woolery." Lennon walks right by me and stops at the game room entrance. Her eyes light up with mischief.

Charlie and I follow, finding Sydney and Brady playing foosball, the two of them joking and laughing with one another.

I take a step in, but Charlie places her hand on my stomach to stop me. Our eyes meet and she silently shakes her head.

"Oh, you got one of those." Lennon knocks shoulders with Charlie. "I'm pretty sure Jasper will be that way with Bianca."

"What way?" Jasper shows up and hands his wife a

coffee. They must've stopped at Steaming Hotties on the way.

"Protective." Lennon nudges her husband and then head nods into the room.

The four of us leave the doorway. Well, Charlie drags me away, but nonetheless, we leave the two tweens alone. Rather irresponsible if you ask me.

"We should get going and let you get settled." Charlie takes the reins, but Lennon moves over to one of her bags. "Charlie." She nods to get Charlie to join her.

"She's going to try to make you be a test subject. Be careful." Jasper warns as she walks over to Lennon. They both disappear with a bag into the laundry room.

"What are you doing?" Jasper hollers to his youngest son, spotting him licking the frosting off each cupcake. "This is your mom's doing, right?"

"I told him to stop." Bianca's shoulders rise and fall. "He never listens to what's good for him."

Jasper points to the dark-haired girl with pigtails. "She's the spitting image of her mother."

He wets a paper towel and wipes down Evan and I notice that his ring finger has an L tattooed on it.

"You guys got tattoos?" I ask.

He stares down to where my finger is pointing.

"Because my fingers got too fat when I was pregnant," Lennon says as the girls join us in the kitchen again. "I couldn't wear my ring so we got tattoos right after I delivered." She eyes her husband and they share a smile.

Jasper covers Evan's ears and Lennon covers Bianca's. "I'm pregnant again," Lennon whispers. "We're telling everyone Christmas morning." She takes her hands off and points to the little ones.

"Congratulations," Charlie says, her smile wide.

"What are you talking about?" Evan asks.

"Mommy having a baby," Bianca says matter of factly then bites into her cupcake again.

I almost choke on my own saliva.

"Bianca! How do you know?" Lennon swivels her head to look at her daughter.

"You really think we can't hear you when you cover our ears with your hands?"

Lennon looks at Jasper and he rolls his eyes.

Time to get out of here.

"Enjoy the cabin. As always if you need anything, call me." I step backward toward the door. "Sydney!" I yell.

"Why don't you leave her here for awhile? Come back and get her in a little bit. They're having fun," Lennon says.

Charlie looks up at me and nods.

"Listen to your woman," Jasper says with a laugh.

I stare long and hard at Charlie whose smile grows wider with amusement knowing how hard this is for me.

"Lennon, please tell Garrett you'll make sure they're visible at all times?" Charlie says not breaking eye contact with me.

"I'll do one better. Bianca?" Lennon calls and her daughter runs over to her side.

"Yeah, Mommy?"

"Go spy on your brother and Sydney."

Bianca runs off and plops down on the couch, chin in her hands.

"See? All taken care of." Lennon smiles at her daughter, giving her a thumbs-up.

I look back at Charlie not so sure about this plan. I like Jasper and Lennon, but they seem extremely busy.

"Sydney, your dad and I are going to come back in a few hours." Charlie ignores my look.

"Okay." She spins the foosball pole and puts her hands up in the air because she scored.

"Sydney's better than you," Bianca says to Brady and Brady rolls his eyes.

Charlie places her hands on my shoulders and spins me around toward the front door.

"Thanks. This gives us the opportunity to shop for her," Charlie softly says to Lennon.

"My pleasure. Brady needs something more to do than take five showers a day."

My boots stop, but Charlie pushes me forward.

"I'm kidding, Garrett," Lennon says, but Charlie laughs behind me. "Here you go." I turn to find Lennon handing Charlie a bag. "Just email me or call me with feedback."

"Lennon, you can't go making everyone a tester for your products," Jasper tells her.

"Oh hush, you never complain."

We walk out to my truck and they stand in the doorway, arms wrapped around each other, waving goodbye.

26

I walk down Main Street enjoying the festive feeling in the air. The streetlights are wrapped in Christmas decorations, the giant tree stands in the middle of the square next to the gazebo, all decorated, and every shop has red, green and white adorning almost every surface.

Christmas season is the third largest after Memorial Day and Labor Day weekends.

The door of the Mad Batter is steamed up and when I step in, the smell of sugar makes my stomach rumble. Not stopping, I head to the back where Ava is taking out Santa Claus cookies from the oven. Some already decorated ones sit on a wire rack on the other side of the room.

"You need some help?" I grab an apron from the back wall and tie it around me.

"Thank you for coming. I have so many special orders." There's flour in her hair and dried cake batter on her apron that says, 'Let me lead you down the rabbit hole.' I have no idea how a parent hasn't reported her yet.

"Nice apron."

She looks down like she forgot what she was wearing it. "A gift from Dane." She quirks up her right eyebrow.

"I'm here. I'm here," Cat says rushing to the back with Lily not far behind. Cat rushes to put her apron on and then bends over to talk to Lily. "Lily, go out front and hand out some samples." Cat goes ahead and arranges some of the Santa cookies on a tray, handing it to Lily.

"Sydney will be here shortly. She can help too."

"Oh, great." Ava wipes her forehead with her forearm. "Toby is with Dane, but they're both coming later."

"What do you need?" Cat asks as Ava slides a rolling pin her way.

"Roll, cut, and bake. I'll decorate."

The three of us get to work and soon Sydney comes in to help out front with Lily. Toby and Dane stop by, but then head right back out to grab dinner for everyone.

"I'm in shock, Charlie. You haven't sampled one item." Ava laughs and they both look at me.

Actually, I'm in just as much awe as them.

"Well, you need all you can get, right?" I joke, although for the first time in forever something sugary doesn't sound good to me.

As Cat and I move onto Christmas tree cookies, my mind starts working. I think about how I've been with Garrett since before Thanksgiving and we've had sex almost every day. Okay, maybe several times a day if we saw each other.

"I'll be right back, I have to pee." I go to the bathroom and pull out my phone. I pull up my period tracking app. Hmm...October eighteenth. No way. I must have forgotten.

I count twenty-eight days from October eighteenth, that would mean I should have gotten it on November fifteenth, but I was already hooking up with Garrett by that time. And I haven't had it since I've been with him.

Two months late?

I bite the inside of my cheek, my eyes fixated on today's date, December twenty-first. Two whole months without a period. My hand falls to my stomach. No. He's had a vasectomy.

I stand up, pocket my cell phone and walk out of the bathroom. As I walk to the sink I shake off the idea of being pregnant. There's absolutely no way. Vasectomies are more effective than the pill. They're a sure thing.

Turning around, I dry my hands with a paper towel.

"Have you girls ever been late?"

Cat shrugs while she continues to stir the batter in the bowl. "Sure, I try my best to always be on time but it's even harder now with Lily. Now I have to make sure she's ready to go, too, and God forbid the socks she wants to wear that day aren't in her drawer. What a fiasco that is. I'm telling you—"

She stops when she looks up at me. I guess she can tell I'm freaked out or something.

"Charlie?" Cat's voice is one of concern.

"I mean late getting your period...from stress or something? Like you just skipped a month." I shrug, trying to play it off and grab a spatula then start taking cookies off one of the trays.

"Oh," Cat says.

"No," Ava adds.

I shoo away the notion. "He had a vasectomy, so I'm not pregnant. It's just weird. I've always been on time."

Ava sits down at the stool that's positioned right at her ass. "Is Garrett the only one you've been with?" I whip my head in her direction and she holds up her hands. "I'm asking because if you're not usually late and you are now then you're most likely pregnant."

"It could be stress, right? That affects your period."

Again, my hand wants to fall to my stomach, but I deny the urge.

"Sure. Stress can affect your period, but a whole two months? I think you should take a test," Ava says. She shrugs her shoulders in a better safe than sorry act.

"Why? I'm not pregnant. I haven't been with anyone else and Garrett got snipped, so that's it. I'll call my doctor. There has to be something else going on. It must be a mistake."

Ava sits up, piping little black belts onto Santa. "Yeah, I'm sure it's nothing."

I catch her eye Cat and they both share let's-just-go-along-with-it look.

THE NEXT DAY, IT'S EIGHT-O-ONE, AND I'M WAITING FOR MY doctor to answer the phone.

"Dr. Chang's office."

"Hi. This is Charlotte Rose."

"Hi, Charlie. It's Lana. What can we do for you?"

Lana is my third cousin and the last thing I need is her to go spreading rumors. The gossip mill will get back to Garrett before I do if it's something bad.

"Hey, Lana."

"I heard you snagged Garrett Shaw. Nice catch."

"Oh...thanks. Um..."

"I don't show you being due for an exam until next July. Is something wrong?"

When did she get this job anyway?

"No. I was just wondering if I could schedule a meeting with Dr. Chang."

I hear her typing away.

"Oh, I get yah. You need to get on birth control. Hold on and maybe I can find a cancellation."

Again, her long fingernails type on the keys, the echo sounding into the receiver.

"Yeah, that's it."

Sure, we'll go with that. Prenatal vitamins or birth control. One or the other, right?

"Oh, score. I got you at three today, but make sure you're on time. I'm squeezing you in really quick."

"Okay, I'll be there. Thanks, Lana."

I hang up and immediately start pacing the floor, my teeth gnawing on the inside of my cheek.

No way. But what other reason could I be so late?

I dial up Dane because I'm supposed to work at the bar with the holiday rush coming in and school being out for break.

"What's up, buttercup?" he answers and I hear the clinking of pots and pans.

"What are you doing?"

"I'm at the bakery with Ava. We've been here all night."

Oh, this is going to make things that much worse. He was probably going to go home to bed. When I left them last night, Ava still had some specialty cakes to make for today.

"I'm sorry. I have some bad news."

"I don't want to hear it if it's about your shift tonight." I hear what I now know is the baking sheets hitting one another in the sink.

"I'm going to be late."

"Charlie. I really need you tonight," he whines and I'm sure it's because he's half tired. Chad's been doing well since I got the counseling job, but I'm his steady Eddy.

"And I'll be there. I'm just going to be late. That's all."

"I need you to be on time."

"Well, deal with it. I'll be there by four." I hang up, unable to hear anymore of his bitching. I do more for that man than anyone else at that tavern. I have my own problems.

A text comes through a few seconds later.

Dane: *See you at four. Don't make it a habit to hang up on me.*
Me: *What are you gonna do, fire me? :P*

I glance at the clock. Ten after eight. Great only six plus hours until I find out if my world is about to change.

THREE O'CLOCK COMES AND I WALK THROUGH DR. CHANG'S office hoping I look normal. There's nothing about me that screams, *I might be pregnant*, right?

I'm here for birth control.

"Charlie!" Lana screams and a few heads turn my way.

"Hey, Lana. I'm here for my appointment."

She leans forward and whispers. "She's almost done with someone and then you're next."

I sign the papers and take care of my co-pay, then sit back down in front of a fan of parenting magazines on the table in front of me.

Don't need those.

The woman across from me doesn't look familiar and I wonder how far she comes from. Dr. Chang is the best OB in three counties and everyone in those three counties delivers at Wet Rock, the closest hospital.

She rubs her belly and there's a child seat next to her with two feet peeking out. She must have a great sex life, having those two so close together. Either that or she's never heard of birth control.

I inwardly cringe at my own thought. Who the hell am I to judge?

If I'd been on the pill I wouldn't be sitting here right now. But it's always made my hormones go crazy and made me feel overly emotional and unstable and since I've been single for so long I didn't think it was necessary. I'm rethinking that now. Like the boy scouts say, always be prepared.

I pull my phone out trying to distract myself from thinking about how I could very well find myself in the same position as she is.

No. You can't. Garrett had a vasectomy.

I grab my cell from my purse intent on playing some mindless game to make the time pass faster and realize I've missed a text from Garrett.

GARRETT: *I MISSED YOU LAST NIGHT. I EVEN HAD A PRESENT for you.*

INCLUDED IN THE TEXT IS A PICTURE OF HIM IN HIS BOXERS with the dick pouch presented like a present with a ribbon to open it.

I smile, fully distracted about sitting in the obstetrics and gynecologists office, hoping I'm not here for the obstetrics part.

Me: *I'll be unwrapping my present tonight. ;)*

Garrett: *I'm already hard just thinking about your mouth wrapping around my cock.*
Me: *Or I could bury it between my tits.*

My entire body starts to hum thinking about tonight.

Garrett: *Who says we can't have both? I almost forgot, I really did get something for you, too.*

He sends over a picture of lingerie that has two flaps that cover the nipple area.

Me: *I imagine you'll just be ripping those flaps off?*

God, I'm practically throbbing between my thighs now.

Garrett: *You know me so well ;)*
Me: *I don't see any panties.*
Garrett: *You don't need any for what I have planned. And FYI, Syd's sleeping at Chloe's tonight.*
Me: *I'll be over right after my shift.*
Garrett: *I'm telling Dane, you're sick. I can't wait that long.*
Me: *You mean your dick can't wait that long...*
Garrett: *I'm not embarrassed to say you're right. This once.*
Me: *Think about what you'd get if you agreed with me more often.*
Garrett: *What can I say, I like your snarky side. Makes my dick hard as steel.*
I laugh and shake my head.

Me: *Now I'm wet.*
Garrett: *Meet me at the Calloway cabin. I'll slide into you in the master bath.*

Me: *Wish I could. I have to work.*
Garrett: *Tonight it is. I'll try to stay up for you, but don't forget to unwrap your present in case I fall asleep...with your teeth.*
Me: *Deal*

"MISS ROSE," THE NURSE ANNOUNCES AND I STARTLE IN MY chair.

"Must have been some great texts." The lady next to me says with a smirk that shows she knows exactly what I was doing.

I give her a small smile and feel the heat rise in my cheeks. "Hi." I stand and greet the nurse who looks like she's even younger than me.

"Afternoon. Third door on your right."

Once we're in the room the nurse takes my blood pressure, weighs me, and tells me to sit down on the bed and Dr. Chang will be right in.

The walls are filled with various posters about birthing —a chart showing how the baby grows month to month, another slew of parenting and prenatal pamphlets. Shouldn't there be separate rooms for obstetrics and gynecology? I need the literature on possible reasons why I haven't had my period, not the three trimesters of pregnancy.

Dr. Chang walks in before I get desperate enough to read one of the pregnancy magazines.

"Hi, Charlie," she says, putting her hand out for me to shake.

"Hi, Dr. Chang."

She takes a seat on the rolling stool. "So, your chart says you're looking for birth control?"

"No. Well, I said that because my cousin is your secretary and I didn't want anyone else to know why I'm really here. Our conversation is confidential, right? Like you can't tell anyone what we discuss?"

Dr. Chang chuckles at my rambling. "Yes. This is just between us. Now, tell me what's wrong?"

"I'm late. Two months late."

She types something into her computer. "Have you taken a pregnancy test?"

"I'm not pregnant."

She quirks an eyebrow. "You haven't been sexually active?" she asks, clearly thinking I'm an idiot.

"I have, but my partner had a vasectomy twelve years ago."

She jots down more notes on her computer.

"And he's your only partner?"

"Yes." God, I'm tired of that question. "Could it be anything else?"

"You're a healthy female, your pap came back normal just a few months ago. I really think the first thing we should do is a pregnancy test." She stands up, taking a cup down from the cabinet.

"Okay, but I think it's a waste of time."

She smiles at me over her shoulder and I get the feeling she's biting her tongue.

"Take this to the bathroom and then place it in the cabinet right next to the mirror after you're done."

I take the plastic cup and walk out of the office and to the bathroom. I sit on the toilet for at least five minutes, wishing I'd drank a gallon of water before coming here. Finally, I'm able to do as she asked and I stick the cup in the cabinet, wash my hands, and go back to my assigned room.

I sit and wait for the doctor to come and tell me I was right and that we'll have to explore some more tests.

Dr. Chang walks in with no expression on her face, which makes me nervous that maybe this is more serious than I first thought. She leans her back on the counter.

My gut twists and churns. This is worse than I thought.

"Charlie. Thank you for taking the test. It's good to always eliminate things when it only means a collection of urine." She pauses. "The reason you haven't had your period is because you're pregnant."

That twisting and churning in my stomach hardens and it drops down to the depths of my stomach.

"No. How?"

"Well, as I'm sure you know, only abstinence is one hundred percent effective at preventing pregnancy. Do you know if your partner sent a sample in after the procedure to make sure it was successful?" She crosses her arms over her chest and waits for me to respond.

I can't though. I can barely form a coherent thought in my mind because she just told me that I'm PREGNANT.

"You always have to go back and make sure you aren't producing any more sperm," she continues on when she realizes I'm not going to respond. "It's not uncommon for men not to follow through with submitting a sample. Happens more than you think."

I shake my head in disbelief. "It all happened before I was in his life."

The nurse knocks on the door and enters with a bag and hands it to the doctor.

"Well, what's done is done. If he's your only partner than he's in the very small percentage where his vasectomy was not effective. In the bag are some brochures about different things like cord blood storage and other promotional things.

Also, there's a prescription for prenatal vitamins. I'd like you to book an appointment for next week and maybe bring in the father so we can get an ultrasound to date the pregnancy."

She pushes herself off the counter and places her hand on my shoulder.

"Congratulations, Charlie." Her smile does nothing to warm my body that is suddenly ice cold and shaking.

I know Garrett and I have been moving fast, but I don't think either of us is ready for this.

Charlie's Jeep headlights light up my window so, I stand to open the door for her.

"Are you here for your present?" I joke, but she walks by me instead and sits on the couch. "You're off early." It's only six o'clock and she was supposed to work until ten.

"I called in sick."

"That a girl. Stick it to Dane." I chuckle.

I plop down on my leather couch and put my arm around her. "Whoa, what's the matter?" It's only now that I get a good look at her face that I realize her eyes are red and bloodshot and a tear trickles down her cheek. "Charlie? What is it?"

My gut clenches as all the worst case scenarios run through my head. Is one of her parents sick? Did something happen to Vance? Did she lose her job at the school?

She looks up at me, tears continuing to roll down her cheeks, but her eyes lock with mine. "I'm pregnant."

"What?"

There's no way I heard that right. She wouldn't do that to me.

"I'm pregnant," she whispers.

My entire body numbs. "How? Whose is it?"

Her sadness morphs to anger. "Yours! Why do people keep asking me that? Like I'm some slut who sleeps around." She brings her legs up to her body and wraps her arms around them.

I stand and start pacing, needing to move—to do *something*.

"It can't be mine. I had a vasectomy. Now tell me who the hell it is so I can go beat the shit out of him right now." I ball my fists up at my sides.

"There is no one else. It's yours. Stop being a fucking Neanderthal."

I stop pacing.

I can see that she's telling the truth and beyond the shock of what she's just told me I feel like a douche for suggesting it could be anyone else's...but I had a vasectomy.

"How is that possible?" I ask.

"Apparently, a vasectomy isn't always one hundred percent effective and you need to go back after three months to see if the procedure worked. To make sure your swimmers are dead." Her tone is accusatory.

"Yeah, well, I'm sure I did that..."

"You're sure. Like you remember going?"

I run my hand down my beard. "I don't remember, *remember*. Sydney was only six months old. That whole time in my life is kind of a blur."

"Did you even have the procedure?" She stands up and moves to the kitchen.

"I think I'd remember some doctor doing surgery through my nuts, yeah." I follow her to the kitchen and watch as she swings open the fridge door, her hand moving from a bottle of beer to a water in the fridge.

"Well, apparently you're a rare breed because it didn't take." She leans on the counter, sipping on her water. "Now we have an appointment next week for an ultrasound and to figure out how far along I am. When I was leaving, the nurse also said they'd probably want to start talking about our birthing plan, too."

Every muscle in my body stiffens. "Birthing plan?"

"Yes, you know when I get to squeeze a watermelon out of my vagina?" Her eyes are wild as they look on at me.

"We should sue the doctor who did the procedure."

I reach in and grab a beer.

Fuck it. It's either this or I'm going to start doing shots.

Her hand slaps the counter. "Focus, Garrett. That ship has sailed. You knocked me up and now we have to figure out how to move forward."

"This can't be happening." I sit down in the chair, set my beer on the kitchen table and place my head in my hands.

"Listen." She sits down, her hand on my bicep. "I know we never planned for this, but there's no going back. We're going to have a baby. Our relationship is new, I get it, but we can make this work."

I pick up my head, tears threatening to fall as they pool in the corners of my eyes. "I honestly don't see how it's mine."

"It? That's how you're referring to *our* baby?"

I stand up and tuck in the chair, my hands white knuckling the back. "It's not ours, it can't be." I walk toward my office.

Smash.

A beer bottle hits the wall right above my head.

"Fuck you, Garrett Shaw. Fuck you!"

Then she's running out of my house and I stare down at the glass shattered into a million pieces on the floor, just like my heart.

CHARLIE

Tears stream down my face, dripping into my lap while snot fills up my nostrils. I need a Kleenex, but since I can barely make out the road now through my tears, taking my eyes away to focus on the glove compartment wouldn't be my wisest decision. Especially since I'm traveling with a little companion now.

I park outside my apartment and my hand falls to my belly, rubbing up and down.

"I'm sorry about Daddy, he's being an asshole," I mumble. "Strike that last word. Bad word. Not nice. Daddy isn't being nice, but he's scared. I knew he would be. But I didn't think he'd disown you."

I take my keys out of the ignition and enter the apartment.

Not having much energy or drive to do anything else, I lie on the sofa and grab the remote.

Clicking on the television, I start my Netflix stream of Gilmore Girls, but then I remember Sydney and I promised to watch it together. So instead, I click on Felicity.

The first episode ends. Guess I'll be watching that again,

because the entire time, my mind is on my baby and my baby daddy.

I guess I shouldn't be that surprised—he's let fear rule his life for the past twelve years. Of course he'd accuse me of sleeping around. It doesn't mean it doesn't hurt any less. It's a good way for him to hate me forever so if something did happen to me in childbirth it wouldn't destroy him. He's blind *and* stupid.

"Sorry little bug, your daddy needs to come to some realizations on his own."

Mental note to self, stop talking to the baby about its daddy.

The door to the apartment swings open. Ava and Cat both come in with brown paper bags of takeout food, unsure expressions on their faces.

"How are you?" Ava asks, kneeling on the carpeted floor and opening the bags.

"I'm fine, why?"

Cat joins me on the couch, her hand rubbing my leg. "So, you're pregnant?" she asks.

I don't turn my head away from the TV, but I move my eyes to look at her from the side. I went straight to Garrett's after a walk in the park how the hell could she possibly know?

"That's an all-time record for Climax Cove gossip ring," I say.

"You called in sick to Dane," Ava says with a frown. "You went in one time with that horrible sinus affection and he had to send you home. After last night, we put it all together." Ava places the quesadilla, rice, beans, and tacos on the coffee table. A whole Mexican feast, which as strange as it sounds, smells amazingly awesome right now, even though I've never been a big eater when I'm upset.

I nod, tears already forming in my eyes. I sit up and Cat wraps her arms around me and Ava joins us.

"It will be fine. I know it's unplanned, but—"

"He doesn't believe the baby is his." The tears becoming too much, I wipe under my eyes, grabbing a napkin from the table.

"What?" Ava asks, her tone flabbergasted and offended even though the accusation wasn't directed at her.

"He thinks it's not possible since he had a vasectomy."

"What a douchebag!" Ava stands and grabs her phone.

Before I can stop her, she's already talking into the receiver. "You need to talk to your friend. He's being a complete asshole." There's a pause. "I don't care. Go over there after work and straighten his shit out. Find out for yourself."

"Ava," I hear Dane saying her name when she clicks off the phone.

"That should handle that." She sits back down, handing out forks.

"We're going Chinese style, just dig in."

We all laugh, using each of our forks to dive into the food.

"I hate to be the one to ask, but are you okay with this? Even if Garrett doesn't want any part of the baby's life?" Cat asks, showing how little she knows him.

"He will. I know he will. He's scared."

"How can you sound so sure when you were just crying about it?" Cat asks.

"I'm upset he accused me of sleeping with someone else, but I know it's all out of fear. I was there twelve years ago...I remember how it destroyed him." I squeeze my eyes shut to stop any more tears from falling because the memory of that time in his life is hard to bear. "*I* know it, but he has to figure it out for himself and learn to handle those fears in a better way."

"Fear of what?" Cat asks.

"Fear of losing the people he cares about. He's not ready to admit to himself that this is happening whether he's scared or not."

"Man, Charlie. You're a rock star." Ava shoves in a spork full of rice into her mouth. "I'd probably just cut Dane's dick off."

I give her a small smile. "No, I'm just an expert on Garrett Shaw."

I won't admit it to the girls, but I damn sure hope I'm right.

Two days of hell...
...of loneliness...
...of starvation from Charlie.

I ENTER HAPPY DAZE TAVERN ON MONDAY FOR THE SINGLE Dad's Club and there she is behind the bar. Should she be on her feet this much?

I approach the bar like a skittish dog from a shelter. She's going to bite my head off, I know it. And I'll let her because I deserve it.

"Charlie."

She puts her hand up in the air. "I'm working."

My shoulders sag.

"Come on. Can we talk on your break?"

"Nope. Would you like a drink?" She never makes eye contact with me.

"No, I want you."

"You had me, Garrett and you chose to toss me away at

the most vulnerable time of my life." I see those tears resurfacing from the other night and I feel sick inside.

"You guys can use my office." Dane nods to the back hallway and I'm all for taking the opportunity, but Charlie moves on to the next customer.

"Looks like you're gonna have to do a lot more than talk." He raises his eyebrows. "Remember what I did to get Ava back?"

"Listen, I'm out for the meeting. I need to figure some shit out."

Dane nods.

"Want some company?"

"Nah, but thanks."

My chin falls to my chest and I leave Happy Daze Tavern with a better understanding of exactly how much damage I've let my fear cause.

I'M NOT SURE HOW I END UP OUTSIDE THEIR HOUSE, BUT MY truck sits in their driveway and I turn off the ignition.

What am I doing? Asking my ex in-laws for advice?

How can I throw it in their face that I get a second chance—one they'll never get.

The front door opens and Violet stands in the doorway, ushering me in with her hand.

Having no other choice, I step out of the truck. My legs feel like lead weights as I trudge up to the front door.

Her arms open and her small frame hugs me as tight as she can.

"I know." Two words from her and I'm thankful for that Climax Cove gossip ring because the words won't have to come out of my mouth. "And it's going to be okay."

She releases her hold on me and we step into the house, passing all the pictures of Melissa on the way.

"Sit down." She points the kitchen table.

"Where's Phil?"

She goes to the refrigerator and pulls out the strawberry dessert she thinks I love. I mean it's okay, but one time when I was dating Melissa I raved about it and now I get it at least once a month when I come over. It's almost as if she's always got it prepared on the off chance I might stop by.

"He's out doing a few errands."

She places the dish in front of me, with a heaping spoon of whipped cream piled on top.

"So news traveled fast," I say.

"I still have my ladies." She gives me a sad smile and props her elbows on the table. "So, is it true?"

Violet has always treated me like a son. I felt grateful to have the in-laws I did when I married Melissa. It's not like Violet hasn't seen me at my worst.

I nod.

"Oh, Garrett. I know what you're thinking and you know the odds. It's highly unlikely anything will happen to Charlie."

I push the plate away from me. "I'm sorry, Violet. I just can't eat."

She slides it to the side, nodding in understanding.

"When you started dating Charlie, did you think she'd want children?"

This is the laughable moment. I wouldn't doubt if Violet tells me what an asshole I am.

"I got a vasectomy after Melissa died, so when I talked about any future possibility of having kids with Charlie, I thought adoption."

She nods again. "That would have been the safe bet, right?"

"Exactly. I freaked out when she told me the news, said it wasn't mine."

She exhales a deep breath and sits back in her chair. "Oh, Garrett."

"I know."

I hear the disappointment in her voice.

"Melissa had a heart defect none of us knew about, honey. The same thing isn't going to happen to Charlie."

I've talked to the doctors a half dozen times. Always the same thing. Rare. Hardly ever goes undetected that long. Almost never happens. But it happened. To my wife. The woman I loved died while she was bringing our baby into the world. She died on a cold slab of metal in an operating room all by herself.

"You love her." Tears fill Violet's eyes. "You wouldn't be this worried if you didn't."

How do you tell the mother of your first love that you would fall apart without the new woman in your life?

"It's okay, Garrett." She looks around the house. "You know why I keep all these pictures of Melissa up?"

"Because you loved her."

She nods. "Yeah, but I don't want to forget her. I don't want to forget one memory with her and these pictures help keep those memories from fading." She leans forward again and places her soft hand on mine. "You're young and you should find love with someone else. You and Melissa shared a lot of memories, and you'll always have those. But it's okay to make new memories worth remembering."

"After she died, I used to be able to hear her voice. I'd be able to repeat full phrases she'd say. I would tell Sydney stories all the time about things we'd done and what her mom was like. Her voice is gone now. I remember our time together, but it almost seems like it was in another life."

"Twelve years is a long time, Garrett." She squeezes my hand.

"What if—"

"Nope." She shakes her head and a tear falls down her wrinkled cheek. "You aren't going to think like that. There are no guarantees in life, Garrett. Yes, the chance that something could happen to Charlie during the childbirth is minute, but there's no one hundred percent guarantee. This baby is coming and Charlie will be in that delivery room when your child is born. So, the question remains, do you want to be by her side no matter what, or do you want to be in the waiting room?"

"By her side." My answer is instantaneous.

She stands taking my dessert with her. "Then I suggest you get out of here and win her back. You're a lucky man. You somehow found two loves of your life in one lifetime."

"I never thought about it like that."

"Did you think you had to love one more than the other?" She looks over her shoulder from the sink.

I did. I know Charlie's worried about being second best to Melissa. I can't deny that I wasn't worried about always comparing the two of them.

"Thanks, Violet." I stand and place my hands on her shoulders. She pats my hands and I kiss her on the top of the head.

"Go get your girl."

I close my eyes for a moment and hear Violet's deep intake of breath.

I'm sure this is hard for her too, but she's always been a mother figure in my life.

I walk past all the pictures of Melissa and out the door,

my shoulders feeling like a little of the weight and guilt has been lifted.

I pick up Syd from her friend Sasha's house once I arrive back in Climax Cove.

She hops in the truck and slams the door.

"Do you want to go to dinner?" I ask.

"No." She crosses her legs and turns toward the window.

"You're not hungry?"

"No."

"Sydney?"

"What?"

"Oh good, you can say more than just no. I was thinking they turned you into a robot."

She looks my way with a scowl. "How could you break up with Charlie?"

My head falls back to the headrest of the truck. At least she hasn't heard about that yet. This time the Climax Cove gossip ring has pissed me off. My daughter should not find out about this from other people.

"It's complicated."

She swivels to face me and I have to admit, I've seen Sydney mad at me. But this time her eyes are practically shooting fireballs at me.

"What's complicated about the fact that you love her?"

"This is grown up stuff, Syd. I can handle it."

She huffs. "Doesn't seem like you're handling it very well."

"Watch the attitude, kiddo."

I put the truck in reverse and drive through downtown Climax Cove back up to our cabin since she's not hungry.

Thinking twice, I make a sharp left and head toward another area. A place I haven't been too much since Sydney was four. I know she's been here with Violet and Phil, but we've never gone together.

We pull into the cemetery and Sydney lets out a long exasperated sigh.

"She's dead, Dad! Charlie is alive and breathing! You have to let Mom go!" she screams.

I'm so caught off guard by her outburst that it takes me a moment to react.

I stop the truck, but Sydney unbuckles her seatbelt and climbs out before I can grab her.

I climb out and follow her down the path.

"Sydney, it's cold. Get in the truck."

She turns around and starts walking away from me, facing me and walking backward.

"Why do you refuse to live your life? You didn't die with her." Another woman I love with tears falling from their eyes because of me.

"Just listen."

"No. I'm done listening. You're going to let a woman who is madly in love with you slip away from you all because you can't get over a dead woman."

"That dead woman is your mother." I point to her and she turns around.

I've always worried I never helped Sydney cope with the fact she never knew her mother. When she was younger, she'd show Melissa's picture around and say, 'This was my mommy. She died'. Now, Sydney never wants to talk about her. I took my cues from her but maybe I should have pressed her to talk about it more.

"Talk to me," I urge but Sydney's dark hair swings back and forth in front of me while she stomps away.

She stops when she reaches her mom's gravesite. It's been years since I've been here, but I still remember the tree that sits beside it. Sydney falls to the ground and her hand brushes along the headstone.

"She'd want you to be happy," she mumbles and I take a seat next to her.

"I know."

"You found happiness with Charlie and now you're messing it all up."

This is when I know I did something right with Syd. She'll sit and talk with me.

"I'm going to win her back. I'm worried about losing another young lady I love."

A small smile forms on her mouth.

"So you admit that you love her?" She glances over at me and I smile.

"Yeah. You happy now?"

"A bit. Are you going to ask her to live with us?" She turns to face me, crossing her legs.

"How would you feel about that?" I pull my knees up to my chest and wrap my arms around them, staring at the lettering of Melissa Shaw carved into stone beside me.

"I know it'll be weird at first, but she makes you smile, Dad."

"I smiled before Charlie."

She quirks her lips and shakes her head. "Not the kind of smiles you do since she's been around."

"Really?"

She giggles and nods her head.

"Come here." I hold my arm out and she slides over to me. Once she's wrapped in my arms, I kiss her temple, still surprised she's so big. "I'm here for you no matter what, okay? I know this is a lot of change."

She smiles. "I'm ready."

"You had a good childhood, right?"

She turns my way, her grin showing the straight teeth from her braces. "The best, but it's not over, Dad. You're still stuck with me for six more years."

"Never stuck. And hey?"

She looks back up to me.

"Don't worry about me. I'm a big boy and I can handle myself." The thought of her wasting any time worrying about my well-being is unacceptable.

"Charlie's the one, Dad. She's our puzzle piece that's been missing."

"How did you get so smart?" I pull her closer and to my relief, she doesn't pull away.

"You and Mom." I nod, closing my eyes briefly.

"Thanks for being such a great daughter. Some girls wouldn't be so understanding about bringing a new woman into our house."

She shrugs. "Thanks for asking me if it was okay. Some dads wouldn't even care what their daughter thought."

We sit for a while, the cold chilling our bones and before we leave, I watch Sydney kiss her fingers and run them over the headstone.

Sydney walks away toward the truck, leaving me alone. After reading her headstone one more time, I rest my hand on the cold granite.

Peace settles over me with my decision to move on and when I walk away from her, the guilt and fear fade away with each step, and I swear I feel Melissa's memory loosen its grip on me.

Now I just need to convince Charlie that I'm done with the fear and that I may be a world-class idiot, but she *has* to take me back.

CHARLIE

Two days before Christmas, and I'm ready to use a hammer to every store that's playing Christmas music. It used to be my favorite, but that's before I became nauseous after everything I ate. It started yesterday and the fact that I don't even want Ava's goods—and by goods, I mean anything comprised mainly of sugar—I'm pissed off.

"Hey, Charlie." Sydney surprises me at my side.

"Oh. Hi, Syd."

Do not ask her about her father. You do not care. He could have fallen down a well at this point and you would not care.

"Can you help me pick something out for my dad?"

We slide between the shoppers and the tourists filling into downtown. Tonight is Climax Cove's big winter festival with Santa, aka, Hank from Nail Me Hardware.

"Right now?"

"Yeah. You know how I barely get out from his thumb. He dropped me off and is letting me go on my own for one hour."

I like Sydney too much to deny her request even though

I'm equal parts enraged and madly in love with her father. "Do you have anything in mind?" I look around, wondering where he's watching her from. Because I know that man and he didn't just drop her and go.

"I figure you might know better than I would."

I shake my head. "Syd, I know you must know. Don't play dumb with me."

"I know he screwed it up. Is it true though...are you pregnant?"

I stop on the spot and lead her over to stand by a nearby bench.

"Please tell me your dad told you?" I say.

She shakes her head. "Nope."

I place my hand on her shoulder. "I'm sorry, Syd. You should have found out from your father."

She shrugs. "It's okay, but you are, right? So, I'm going to be a big sister?"

I nod, unable to hide my smile. "You are."

She rushes toward me, wrapping her arms around my shoulders. "Please take him back. I know he's stubborn, but I know he loves you." I close my eyes at her words, hoping that her dad will come to the same realization she has.

"This is for you." She hands me a letter and then she's gone, lost in the crowd walking away.

My name is scribbled on the outside of the letter in Garrett's handwriting, and I sit down on the bench.

I open the heavy envelope, finding a puzzle piece inside, along with a letter.

Charlotte,

You will receive three letters today. The first might be hard to read, but I do hope you continue on.

Melissa was my first love, first kiss, first everything. The two of us grew up together. Although there are times I wonder what our future would have looked like, I can't say for certain. What we were when she passed is all we will ever be. It took me years to finally come to grips with the fact that nothing will ever change that.

I can't offer you those firsts because they were already given to someone else. Someone I loved deeply. Someone who gave me my daughter. That is a part of my life you weren't a part of, but it was a happy time in my life and I can't ever deny that fact or look back on it with anything other than fond remembrance.

But I have memories of you, too. Memories of you riding your bike, your scraped knees, the way you used to hang around and trail after us even when Vance tried to get you to go home. Summer trips to the pool, eating popsicles on your front porch, playing games outside on summer nights. Though our relationship wasn't romantic and you were years younger, you are still a part of my past.

If I could do it all over again I'd have sat with you longer on your front porch, listened to your dreams and never have let Bobby Sinclair pull your pants down that one time at the park.

If you're interested in continuing, your next letter will be delivered in an hour.

Love,

Garrett

I FOLD THE PIECE OF PAPER AND STUFF IT IN MY POCKET ALONG

with the puzzle piece. I appreciate the honesty in his letter. Although I've struggled with being second best, Melissa was part of his life and that fact won't ever change. So, either I welcome her memory into our relationship, if only for Sydney's sake, or we'll never make it long term. She's Sydney's mom and his dead wife. There has to be room for them to remember her in our lives and I'm happy he's embracing that fact rather than denying it. For me, it signals a shift and I can only hope that he's ready to tackle the past, present, and the future head-on now.

I'M IN STEAMING HOTTIES, GRABBING A GREEN TEA BECAUSE I can't drink caffeine. Argh. Who said pregnancy was fun?

"Hey," Ava and Cat say in unison, sitting down at the table with me.

"Are you my second letter?" I ask and Ava tries to keep a straight face while Cat smiles.

I hold out my hand. "Not yet," Ava says. She turns her head sharply to Cat. "You're hopeless. You know that, right?"

"I just want them to get back together." Cat claps her hands like a seal.

I roll my eyes and push my hand closer to Ava.

"You are seriously no fun." She digs it out of her purse and slides it across the table.

"Is he watching?" I lean closer and whisper.

Ava does the same. "No."

"Really?" My lips tip down.

"Stop asking questions. You'll ruin the surprise. This is his big moment to woo you back and right his wrongs. Enjoy it." Ava leans back, glancing at the bakery display, probably checking on her own inventory.

"Yeah, because the wooing stops pretty quick after they've caught you," Cat says with some humor to her voice, crossing her legs and watching me open the letter.

My finger runs along the seam.

"Maybe I don't need wooing," I say like my stubborn self.

The two exchange a look but then smile on at me.

Charlotte,

The greatest gift in my life has always been Sydney. I can't deny that she's number one in my life, but she's going to be in a tie with our little one soon.

I watch you with Sydney and my heart bursts open like an explosion of confetti. She needs a mother figure, and I can think of no one better than you...someone she feels comfortable talking with about things I'll never understand or relate to, someone to watch Gilmore Girls with, someone to initiate family traditions that she'll carry on to her own family some day. She's grown to love you.

She's not the only one though. You might worry that it's only your body I crave, which I do. I'd put dirty words in here, but I'm worried you'll keep this in a box and our kids will read it one day. Let's just say...your physical appeal is only a small part of what makes you irresistible. It's your heart, your patience, and your persistence, too.

I regret not seeing what was right in front of my face sooner. But these last months with you...I feel like my old self. I feel like the future is bright and anything is possible. For the first time, for as long as I can remember, I'm excited for the future and what it might bring, not burdened by the past and fearful of what might come. That is the most precious gift you'll ever give me...until our son or daughter arrives.

You'll need a ride for your next trip, so, be prepared to be picked up in one hour.

Love,
Garrett

I swipe the tear that's fallen down my cheek.

"Okay, gotta go." Cat stands, having never taken off her coat. She leans down and gives me a half hug and kiss on the cheek.

"Forgive him, Charlie. He knows what he did." Ava does the same as Cat with a small hug and kiss on the cheek.

"Bye, girls."

I sit down and sip my tea, before folding the paper and stuffing it in my pocket.

I rest my hand on my stomach and murmur, "I think your daddy might just be ready for us."

I'm gazing up at the Christmas tree in the middle of the downtown courtyard when someone takes my hand and pulls me away.

"Hey," I pull back to see Vance.

"Hey, little sister." He smiles and reaches for my arm. "I'm your chauffeur for the evening."

"After everything he did, you're doing him a favor?"

He opens up the passenger seat of his rental car and waits for me to sit down.

"If you're staying in Climax Cove, you better get rid of this car."

He shuts the door and rounds the front to the driver's side.

"I'm heading back to L.A. in the morning. It's time I go back."

I'll miss my brother, but he's never been one for small-town living.

"Really, on Christmas Eve you're leaving?" I whine.

"I promise to visit more often. I'll have to since I'm getting a niece or a nephew in the new year." He smiles and turns the key in the ignition.

"You better. Otherwise we're coming down to see you."

He drives slowly through the streets cluttered with people and turns the car down my parents' street.

"Why are we going to Mom and Dad's?"

"Relax. They're in downtown for the festival. I'm just following orders. I was told to drop you off here."

He stops in my parents' driveway, hands me a letter, and then reaches across and opens the passenger door.

I spot Garrett's truck parked on the street and I realize how anxious I am to see its keeper.

"Thanks, Vance." I lean forward and kiss his cheek.

"I told him this is his second strike, one more and I'll have to kick his ass. It's my brotherly duty."

I smile. "Thank you."

"Go live the life you've always wanted, sis." He ushers me out and then he's quick to back up and drive away.

I'll miss him.

For the third time, I slide my finger along the seam of the letter and unfold the piece of paper.

Charlotte Rose,

My future begins today. My future is you. In the first letter, I talked about how you weren't able to be a part of all my firsts, but what matters most, I think, is that I want you to be a part of all my lasts.

My last kiss, my last love, my last mother to my child.

I can't take back the way I acted when you told me you were carrying our child. If I could I would because you deserve better. You both deserve better. I should have hugged you and reassured you that we'd get through this together. I freaked out, but I want you to know that it's only because I love you...because the thought of losing you is too devastating to even consider.

I could list five hundred reasons why I fell so deeply and madly in love with you, but the reason that was the tipping point is that you saw the true me and never gave up on trying to pull me back to the surface. Looking back I realize that you've never given up on me, even when you were a graduating senior writing that essay that came to mean so much to me. But, I gave up on you, on us, if only for a moment.

Sorry will never be enough and I know that. But, you have my solemn promise that it will never happen again. I refuse to live my life on the sidelines any longer, refuse to let fear have any power over my decisions. The only way for me to prove that to you is throughout the course of our lives together.

You pulled me from the depths of depression not once but twice, now it's my turn to have the strong shoulders and do the heavy lifting. I promise to be the father of this family we're developing and be strong enough to hold everyone up.

If you still believe in me, step through that front door so we can start again at the beginning of what will be our last.

Come to me, baby.

Love Always,
Garrett

I fold up the letter and turn the doorknob of my childhood home. I walk through the house and in the kitchen sits Garrett at the table, candles lit all around him.

"Hey." He stands and rounds the front of the table.

"Hey."

"You got them all?"

I nod.

"Do you have the puzzle piece?"

I nod, digging into my pocket to retrieve it. I hold it up and he looks at it warily for a moment before he begins speaking again.

"This is where your words changed me as a man and a father. Your mom gave me that paper right here, eight years ago. And if you would have taken me back easily, I never would have realized this."

He takes a towel off a puzzle on the kitchen table.

There's a picture of Melissa in the top left corner and then one of him and Sydney and lastly me on the far right. It was taken at the tree lighting ceremony a few weeks ago.

"Sydney said something to me...she said that you were the missing puzzle piece to our future. I love you, Charlotte Rose and I want you to fill that void and be my future."

I twirl the puzzle piece around in my fingers and he studies me the entire time, his posture stiff and looking like he's barely breathing.

Slowly, I insert it in the open spot, and the puzzle is complete.

Relief washes over all his features. "You forgive me?" he asks.

I nod with tears in my eyes and he hugs me, squeezing me tight and I feel at home again. Almost as if all the pieces of myself have been slotted back into place where they should be.

After a few minutes, Garrett places his hand on my stomach and falls to his knees.

"I can't wait to meet you, little one. You were a shock, but the best surprise I've ever had in my life. Now, has Mommy been saying bad things about Daddy?" He glances up at me and I roll my eyes, but I'm sure from my smirk he can tell that I have. "Well, it's all true, but don't you worry because Daddy is changing every day."

I chuckle. "Come here."

Then I grab his face with both my hands and place my lips to his knowing that nothing will ever tear us apart again.

Two Weeks Later ...

Tomorrow is the first day back to school after holiday break and I'm struggling to get all my things organized after moving in with Garrett and Sydney on Christmas Eve. My life is in a bit of a shambles lately and presently I'm missing my messenger bag with my computer in it.

I feel like I've been in la-la land as of late, lost in Garrett's world for the past few weeks. Not that I'm complaining—Garrett's world is a pretty damn awesome place to me.

Garrett walks in with a bag in his hand and places it on the bed.

"What did you get?" I ask.

"It's a gift for you." He moves to his dresser, not really

paying that much attention or seeming to bother with watching me open the bag.

"Jeez. It's been two weeks since you gave me a gift. I understand what Cat and Ava were talking about with the lack of wooing once you get together," I joke. I sit on the mattress and pick up the bag.

He doesn't say much, and his back is to me, so I start taking the tissue paper out.

I grab the heavy item out of the bag and smile, even though I'm a little confused.

He got me a new placard for my desk that says Charlotte Shaw. I never realized how nice that name sounds.

I look up and there he is on bended knee in front of me holding up a box with a large diamond ring inside.

I suck in a breath and my stomach lurches. "Garrett." I cover my mouth, and the thought that I wish I was in anything but yoga pants and a T-shirt flits through my mind.

"See," he winks. "I can still woo."

"You can." Tears spring to the corners of my eyes.

He scoots forward. "Charlotte Rose, I know it seems crazy and too fast but I promised myself that fear would never hold me back anymore...marry me."

"Is that all you have to say?" I hold the placard up that has what will be my married name. "Pretty presumptuous of you."

He chuckles, not faltering from his position. "I'm a man of few words."

I shake my head. "Oh, I don't think so."

"Well, not anymore."

I smile.

"Charlie?"

"Yeah?"

"Answer the question."

I look right into the set of eyes I've dreamed of half my life.

"Yes, nothing would make me happier than becoming your wife."

He exhales a relieved breath. "Thank God. Now, Sydney is coming back in one hour. Get naked."

"How romantic." I fall to my back and he slides the diamond on my left ring finger.

"Perfect. Now you're even sexier with my ring on your finger."

"What's going to happen when I'm too swollen from being pregnant to wear it?"

"You'll still be sexy as hell."

I hold it up in the air and then look to him, hovering over me. "I love you."

"I love you more, Charlie. Thanks for sticking with me until I was smart enough to realize it."

EPILOGUE

GARRETT

The Following Summer...

The girls are watching television and I'm in the kitchen cooking dinner. It's a lazy Sunday afternoon. Charlie's due any day and she's swollen from the heat of the hottest summer on record.

"Look at the plans, Charlie," I yell out from the kitchen because the architect wants the final draft back to him tomorrow in order to finalize the plans for our new house. One that includes a nursery.

"Dad, I think I need a bigger closet," Syd yells out.

"You don't."

"I do."

"Sydney, you don't."

"I think she might," Charlie replies and I'm happy that means she's actually looking at it. My wife hasn't done anything other than 'nest' these past few weeks and trying to nail down these plans has been a challenge.

Yeah, I said wife. After I proposed and she accepted we decided we didn't want to wait to make it official. We had a small ceremony in the winter to officially begin our lives together.

"Dad?" Sydney calls.

"Your brother needs a room, Sydney, unless you want to share yours with a newborn." I round the corner to point to the blueprint when Sydney's pale face alerts me that something's wrong.

My heart kicks into overdrive and I run over to find Charlie gripping Sydney's hand tightly in hers.

"Contraction?" I ask her.

She nods.

"Ew!" Sydney screams at the water covering the brown leather sofa.

"Sydney, get the bag by the front door and turn off the stove and the oven." I round the sofa. "You'll be fine, baby."

I reassure her while even though I feel my own panic setting in.

I slowly help her to the front door.

"Oh, Garrett, we're not ready," Charlie says, some of her dark curly hair coming loose from her ponytail.

"We are. The car seat is in. His room is all ready. We're all set."

She looks at me with worried eyes and I know what she's thinking.

"I'm good, baby, do not worry about me during this." I get her down the steps and into my truck. Running back inside, I scream, "Sydney, let's go!"

She runs down the stairs, grabbing the overnight bag on the way.

"What took you so long?" I take the bag from her and we both run to the truck.

"I had to put on mascara."

I roll my eyes. "Do you think Justin Bieber is going to be there?"

We both file into the truck as I'm saying it.

"Garrett, Bieber is out." Charlie can even find it within herself to correct me while she's in labor.

"I never know who I'm going to see."

"Charlie is in labor. You don't need to be trolling for boys."

The tires of my truck squeal as I reverse down the driveway.

"Trolling?" Charlie cocks her eyebrow at me, looking at me through the corner of her eye.

"Aren't you in labor?"

She giggles. "I am, but right now I feel pretty good." Her hands touch her stomach. She shifts her body. "Once we get to the hospital, remember to send the group text to everyone, Sydney."

"Why does everyone have to be there?" I ask for the thousandth time.

"Because they're family. It'll only be you and Sydney with me through the delivery." I grip the steering wheel tighter, my anxiety creeping up with the thought of Charlie in labor.

When I glance in the rearview mirror Sydney smiles and I'm thankful she'll be in there with us.

You know, in case I pass out or have an anxiety attack or something.

The drive to Wet Rock feels like both an eternity—because I just want to get there so that Charlie is where she needs to be should something happen—and a microsecond—because I also want to prolong the inevitable.

I pull up outside the hospital doors and park, barking an

order at Syd to grab a wheelchair for Charlie. She does as instructed and runs inside the hospital.

"Here, baby let me help you down." I reach out and take Charlie's hand, helping her shift to face me then grip her under the shoulders and lift her from the truck, setting her gingerly on the ground.

"That was a little much," she says and shakes her head.

"Dad, I've got the wheelchair," Sydney says breathlessly from behind me.

I look at her over my shoulder. "Bring it here."

She wheels it over and I help Charlie navigate her large belly into the chair.

"Oh, jeez," Charlie says and reaches for my hand.

"Contraction?" I ask.

She nods frantically and tries to breathe properly.

Sweat breaks out on my brow as I wait for it to pass. She's squeezing the life out of my hand, but I don't care.

"Okay, that wasn't much fun," she says when the pain has passed and let's go of my hand.

"Syd, I need you to wheel Charlie into the labor and delivery wing. I'm gonna park the truck and I'll be right back."

Sydney nods her consent but she's biting her lip so I know she's nervous. She glances from me to Charlie and back again before she takes a deep breath and moves to stand behind the wheelchair.

I look down at the woman who is my whole life because she brought me back to life.

"I'll be quick. Don't you dare have that baby without me." I plaster a smile on my face that belies how anxious I am and lean down and kiss the top of her head.

"Of course not. I can't be screaming and cursing at Sydney while I'm pushing. That's what you're for." She smiles and squeezes my hand before Syd starts pushing her inside.

I park the truck quickly and start walking back toward the hospital. I'm halfway through the parking lot when it hits me—what I'm about to go through...what I've been through before.

Nausea eats at my stomach and my legs start to feel weak. I stop in the middle of the lot to heave in a deep breath.

I can do this. Charlie can do this.

Tears prick the corners of my eyes as a flurry of images bombard my mind. Charlie frightened and frantic during her labor, the doctor saying something is wrong, the nurse pushing me out of the way so they can wheel her into the operating room, Charlie's limp hand hanging over the side of the operating table—

Tears drip into my beard and bring me back to the present.

No. No. No. No. No.

I drag air into my lungs even though it feels almost impossible to do so.

The thought of anything happening to her cripples me. I know I wouldn't recover. I know I couldn't move forward even with two children to care for.

God, if you're listening I know I probably don't deserve anything from you but if you could please watch out for Charlie and my son...help them be strong. Hell, help me be strong. Shit. Sorry for saying the H-E double hockey sticks word. That probably wasn't good. Anyway, please let this be an easy labor and delivery and please keep them safe. I promise I'll make it my mission to be the best father and husband I can be.

I straighten up and wipe the tears from my face feeling better that I've asked a higher power for help. I may not be a religious man, but everyone can use a little help every once in awhile.

I begin walking toward the hospital again with a renewed resolve. Whatever Charlie needs I'm here for her. And right now, I need to be strong for both my wife and my son.

———

A HALF HOUR LATER, WE'RE IN THE BIRTHING ROOM. CHARLIE'S eating ice chips and she and Syd are watching some show set in Alaska.

Like the two of them could ever live off the grid.

Dr. Chang comes in and rolls her chair between Charlie's legs.

"You're progressing great, Charlie, but your contractions aren't quite close enough together to really get things going. I'll be back in an hour or so to see how you're doing." She squeezes her foot and walks out of the room.

So we sit some more. My feet start tapping, my gaze set on Charlie, who is laughing with Sydney about whatever stupid TV show they're watching now.

Don't either of them see how serious this is?

An hour later, Dr. Chang comes back in. "You've dilated some more." She looks at the screen. "Your contractions are getting there. About every fifteen minutes."

Charlie smiles over to me and then to Dr. Chang. "Yeah."

"I'll be back," Dr. Chang says and disappears again.

"Look, we still get a lazy Sunday." Charlie looks between Syd and I.

She's done so well when she does have her contractions and right now she's as cool as can be while she sucks away on her ice chips while the tension in my body just keeps increasing. I just want this over with.

Another hour goes by and my girls are still enthralled with the TV and I'm beginning to grow annoyed with how casual they're being in this situation.

"Ow," Charlie grips the railing of the bed and her body tenses.

"What is it? Are you okay?" I stand up and let her take my hand instead of the railing.

Sydney stands and places her hand on her shoulder.

A couple seconds go by and her body falls to the bed.

"Just a contraction."

We all sit down, but it's not even five minutes later and the same thing happens.

Charlie looks up at me and it's the first time that there's fear in her eyes.

"Sydney, page the nurse on that remote." I let Charlie squeeze my hand until it's numb.

The nurse walks in ten minutes and three contractions later.

"Her contractions seem to be getting stronger and coming closer together," I say, but the nurse just moseys on over to the screen to check things out.

"I'll call the doctor," she says and walks away without any urgency in her step.

Charlie continues to contract, each one growing worse than the one before it.

"Are you guys having me in here for some safe sex thing?" Sydney asks, clearly becoming distraught with the whole process.

"Where is the doctor?" I ask.

Sydney feeds her ice chips and I let her use my hands as her own personal stress ball.

Dr. Chang walks in, rolls herself between Charlie's legs, and then peeks her head out. "You're a slow starter but you're galloping toward the finish line. Feel ready to push?"

Charlie nods frantically and then the doctor stands and leaves the room.

"What the fuck?" I ask.

"Garrett," Charlie admonishes me but I don't care at this point.

Dr. Chang returns a minute later with a team of two nurses.

"It's go time," she says.

The room closes in on me and the corners of my vision becomes blurry. I've been here before.

"Okay, Charlie, give me one long push for ten seconds."

My hand is in hers, she's squeezing while rising from the bed to use all the energy she has.

"Ten, nine, eight, seven, six, five, four, three, two. Good Charlie, good. Now relax," the doctor says.

The pressure on my hand loosens, but it feels like someone dumped a fifty-pound weight on my chest. It's hard to breathe.

"Dad?" Sydney calls my name and I look over at her, finding a weird expression on her face. "Are you okay?"

I nod. "I'm good." Charlie's staring up at me and I know she sees it, too. I was naive to think she wouldn't.

She takes my hand in hers. "We're all good, baby. All of us will be going home with you. Oh, fuck!" she screams and Sydney laughs.

"Okay, push again, Charlie." A nurse brings up her leg on Sydney's side and Syd slides up toward Charlie's head. "And relax."

Dr. Chang's voice becomes muffled in my head. "Okay,

Charlie, the head is out, now I only need one really, really good push to get the shoulders out."

"Fuck." Charlie's gaze zeros in on me. "Never again, you hear me? That vasectomy is happening again and you *will* get tested." Her entire body pries off the bed and the veins in her neck pop out. "We're doing the pill, condoms, IUD and a vasectomy!" She keeps rattling off things until her entire body collapses and the sound of a crying baby rings through the room.

The fog around me lifts.

The walls retract and I stare down at a sweaty and exhausted Charlie.

We did it. She did it.

She places her hand on my cheek and stares into my eyes. "You go with the baby, remember?"

"No." I shake my head. I can't leave her now.

"Yes. I'm fine Garrett, just tired."

A nurse brings the baby over for Charlie to kiss his head and then they're gone.

"We'll be right back with him. Dad?" the nurse says, wheeling our new addition out of the room.

"I'll stay with her Dad," Sydney assures me and I bend down to kiss her head.

"You were amazing, kiddo."

"So were you."

I jog out of the room, following my baby.

My baby! I have a son.

Welcome to the world, Jackson Charles Shaw.

Tears of joy and relief well in my eyes as I wait impatiently for the nurses to conduct the tests and check him out before we can head back to the room.

When we arrive I see that Charlie's eyes are closed.

"She just fell asleep," Sydney says, but I look at her monitor to make sure she's good just in case.

LATER THAT NIGHT, AFTER EVERYONE HAS VISITED JACKSON and Charlie, I slide in next to my wife as she cradles our baby.

"How much better are you breathing now?" Charlie giggles, kissing our son's head.

"I'm all good. Remember the letters I gave you back around Christmas?" My hand runs along her hairline.

"How could I forget?"

"This is a first. I thought I was done with firsts, but this, sitting here and sharing our newborn child together is a first." I kiss her temple, my hand resting on my son's back.

She smiles up at me with tears dotting the corners of her eyes. "You're still wooing me."

"I like to keep you on your toes." I kiss her temple again. It's like I can't stop, I'm just so grateful to be sitting here with her and our son.

"Now, watch out there, Jackson. You may be making use of your mommy's boobs this year, but make no mistake that those babies are mine once you're done with them."

Charlie shakes her head. "They aren't yours again for at least six weeks buddy."

"Six weeks for what?"

"Six weeks until we can have sex."

"Who makes that rule?" I wrinkle my forehead.

"My body has to heal, so Dr. Chang will have to clear us first."

A disgusted look crosses my face and she giggles.

"All right then buddy, you get six weeks. Six weeks until sex weeks."

I waggle my eyebrows and Charlie laughs, causing Jackson to let a wail rip from his newborn lungs.

Never has there ever been a sweeter melody than those two sounds.

The End

COCKAMAMIE UNICORN RAMBLINGS

In the previous ramblings in the back of the Single Dad Club books, we've discussed the photographs we bought from Wander Aguiar for the series covers. How we found Marcus first, Garrett second and Dane third. Truth be told, Rayne wasn't entirely hot on Garrett. No offense to the gorgeous model, Jacob Rodney, but Rayne likes the clean- cut type. Piper LOVED him and how big and burly he was. Then we showed them to Shawna Gavas, (who many of you know is our assistant) and she said she wanted to marry him. So, Jacob Rodney was Garrett Shaw from that point forward in our minds.

Once again, Rayne did the writing after we plotted together and Piper did the editing. Which meant that Rayne had to find Garrett's voice. Like Dirty Talker, the cover of Sexy Beast was plastered on the right side of her computer while she wrote. She kept going back to Piper, wondering how she was supposed to find a man's voice who hardly talked in the first two books. LOL That strong silent type is hard to figure out.

Yes, Garrett's voice was hard to find, but once we did, we knew that he loved Melissa and that didn't mean he couldn't love Charlie with equal weight. We both feel as though this is what makes their story realistic. This is what makes the emotions so raw in their story.

We realized about midway into book one that it was hard to bring humor into this series. There are kids and families involved, we can't go making the parent's irresponsible. So our job was to make it funny, but to do it in a way that someone who spends any time around children could appreciate. The Single Dads Club Series might not be as funny as our Modern Love Series, but we fell in love with each couple just as hard. The town of Climax Cove makes us tempted to write more in this series. **Would you like to see more single dads? If so, reach out and let us know!**

The same as with previous two books in the series, without the help of the following people in our corner we wouldn't have released this book...

Letitia from RBA Designs for the amazing covers and for putting up with how nitpicky we can be.

Ellie from Love N Books for line editing. Earning her nickname Speedy Ellie again this time around.

Shawna from Behind the Writer for her eagle eye proofreading skills and turning this around super fast.

Enticing Journey Book Promotions for their organization and helping us out with all the Single Dads Club Series.

All the bloggers who carved out time to promote us and/or read and review the book.

Michelle New for yet another set of awesome graphics.

Our first readers of a really shitty, unedited copy—Heather and Angela.

Christine from Type A Formatting for such a pretty paperback.

All our early ARC readers, first for wanting to read our stuff early and for posting their reviews.

And of course, all our unicorns. We can't even thank you enough for everything. To making the unicorn group so active and always sharing the latest unicorn paraphernalia to promoting our books and posting how much you love our stories. With us only being on the block for less than year, you've faithfully followed us through two series. We have no words except for thank you and we know that's not enough! You are our mojo!

Our new series, Dirty Truth, is coming Fall 2017, Vance is leading the heroes in book one. You'll find out if his life in Los Angeles is really as glamorous as he makes it sound.

Lastly, Piper had a full circle moment today when she dropped her son off at camp. The same camp that was the impetus for this entire series. And FYI – the camp counselors are still just as cute as last year. 😉 Oh, to be twenty-one again. It seems fitting that on the week the final book in the series is releasing, she returned once again to the place it all began.

We can't wait to bring you more book boyfriends to add to your list! Until then!

. . .

XO,

Piper & Rayne

ABOUT THE AUTHOR

Piper Rayne, or Piper and Rayne, whichever you prefer because we're not one author, we're two. Yep, you get two USA Today Bestselling authors for the price of one. Our goal is to bring you romance stories that have "Heartwarming Humor With a Side of Sizzle" (okay...you caught us, that's our tagline). A little about us... We both have kindle's full of one-clickable books. We're both married to husbands who drive us to drink. We're both chauffeurs to our kids. Most of all, we love hot heroes and quirky heroines that make us laugh, and we hope you do, too.

Goodreads
Facebook
Instagram
Pinterest
Bookbub
www.piperrayne.com

Join our newsletter and get 2 FREE BOOKS!
http://bit.ly/2tsNcpP

Be one of our UNICORNS and join our Facebook group!

ALSO BY PIPER RAYNE

The Modern Love World

Charmed by the Bartender

Hooked by the Boxer

Mad about the Banker

The Single Dad's Club

Real Deal

Dirty Talker

Sexy Beast

Hollywood Hearts

Mister Mom

Animal Attraction

Domestic Bliss

Bedroom Games

Cold as Ice

On Thin Ice

Break the Ice

Box Set

Charity Case

Manic Monday

Afternoon Delight

Happy Hour